Guardians of the Light

Jasper Cross

Contents

Prologue

Walking through rugged metal hallways was a large Cabal in white and gold armor, three strips of red cloth flowing down his back, flanked by faux white wings. He wore a mask over his face, albino white with piercing red eyes. He had a large sidearm on his hip, matching the colors of his armor. He stepped through a large door into a throne room of some kind of warship. There was another Cabal there in red armor, a cape of scales barely scraping against the floor behind him, blind in his scarred left eye. The white armored one lets out a grunt before speaking.

White; "Consul."

The Consul gave a curt bow as the viewport went from opaque to transparent, giving the pair a view of the Earth from high orbit, old satellites crashing against the hull, leaving it undamaged.

Consul; "Dominus Ghaul... Emperor white and gold suits you."

Ghaul scowls as more ships begin entering the periphery of the observation window, at least a score of them.

Ghaul; "Enough pleasantries and compliments, Iago. I'm here for one reason only, and I intend to make this a clean operation."

Ghaul turned to a Psion that had entered the room, wearing armor the same vermillion as Iago.

Ghaul; "Sizmic, get the satellites offline and deploy cyber warfare measures."

The Psion nodded before vacating the room, the viewports beginning to glow with the heat of entering atmosphere, passing into a large storm cloud once the hull began to cool. Iago stood at Ghauls side as the thunder quietly roared outside the ship, lightning flashing occasionally.

Ghaul; "Hmph... The weather works in our favor for once."

Iago let out a singular, haughty laugh, looking to Ghaul with a meager smile; the best a Cabal face could muster.

Iago; "You're the emperor now, my boy! All things bend to your will. The-"

He's interrupted by a groaning alarm coming from the throne, an orange light flashing on the right arm rest. Ghauls expression softened and he hastily made his way to the throne, sitting in it as a holographic projection of a Cabal with tusks protruding from either side of their hooded face, adorned with a pale gold harness and a navy blue loin cloth over a loose shirt, their boots also pale gold. Ghaul spoke to her with a softer voice, as though a teacher speaking to a student.

Ghaul; "Caiatl."

Caiatl straightened her posture when she heard the voice of Ghaul, as though she could only hear him and not see him.

Caiatl; "Dominus. I take it you've arrived in Sol?"

Ghaul adjusted himself in his seat, throwing the strips of crimson cloth behind the throne.

Ghaul; "Indeed, we have. And what of Calus?"

Caiatl glanced over her shoulder before replying.

Caiatl; "My father and the Leviathan have entered FTL speeds; he is no longer in the Torobatl system."

One could imagine a smile creeping up on Ghauls face.

Ghaul; "Very good, young one. I knew you would be the one to take care of the home world in my absence."

Caiatl folded her arms over her chest, lifting her head so her tusks were at the same level as her eyes, said eyes a glowing amber color.

Caiatl; "Do you intend to bring this great machine back to Torobatl with your victory? Or will you carry it with your fleet into battle?"

Ghaul shrugged with a grunt as the clouds ahead began to thin.

Ghaul; "I will decide while the cage is under construction. Stay strong, princess. I will return victorious, or not at all."

Caiatl nodded as the hologram faded, the storm clouds giving way to the Traveler lazily hovering over a city bordered by an immense wall, a large tower ahead of them. Ghauls grip tightened on the arm rests as a communication came through from another Cabal.

Cabal; "Dominus, that tower appears to be their command center."

Ghaul replied with a knitted brow.

Ghaul; "Open fire, low yield warheads. Make them suffer."

Cabal; "All ships focus fire on the tower."

A deluge of rockets poured into the tower, causing explosions all throughout the upper structure, prompting Ghaul to huff in amusement.

Cabal; "Dominus, the citys anti-air defenses are still online; the Psion virus was countered swiftly!"

Ghaul groaned quietly as an even more immense ship passed overhead, harmlessly absorbing the anti-air fire as it expanded into a six pointed star shape, glowing a yellow-ish orange at the rear thrusters.

Ghaul; "Hmm... Someone was expecting us, it would seem. Have the Immortal circumnavigate the tower, the rest of the fleet shall keep the ground forces occupied until the cage can be erected."

Cabal; "What about an assault on the cage, sir?"

Ghaul chuckled as he stood, approaching the window.

Ghaul; "They wouldn't dare fire on their precious Traveler. We need only occupy them long enough to take their power... Then, victory is certain. Deploy squadrons to the tower!"

Cabal; "Yes, Dominus."

Ghaul watched the cage attach itself to the Traveler and begin expanding; long wires of metal and machinery to encircle the sphere. He lost sight of it as the ship moved to circle the tower clockwise, the boom of guns and drop pods being launched filling the observation deck.

Ghaul; "Get me a view of the tower."

The window fizzled with static, the view changing to the starboard side of the ship, circling around to the opposite side of the tower; the side facing the Traveler. He crossed his arms over his chest as the tower was broadsided with missiles and drop pods.

Cabal; "Sir, Psions on the ground are intercepting a transmission."

Ghaul; "Patch it through."

The voice that came over the thrones speaker was Human, feminine but stern and laced with worry, a twang of desperation as well.

"Zavala, the last of the shuttles is away; but the Speaker... He never made it. I'm going to look for him."

Ghaul growled quietly as the transmission cut out.

Ghaul; "Have any Psions detected this "Speaker?" If not, begin searching immediately!"

Cabal; "They're on the hunt, sir... Dominus, the Glykon Volatus is picking up a Human ship departing for orbit. Ground troops say they've captured Ixel."

Ghaul clenched his fists with a mix of a growl and a hiss.

Ghaul; "Send a Cruiser after them. Wherever they go, deploy fortifications and begin mining operations. Prepare construction for a shipyard as well; I'd rather not have all our forces kept exclusively on Earth."

Cabal; "Understood, sir."

Iago came alongside Ghaul once more as a shadow of a ship passed across the window, its silhouette barely visible through the screen.

Cabal; "Dominus, they've deployed a Human on the starboard landing pad."

Iago scoffed and turned to look at Ghaul.

Iago; "Just one?"

Ghaul; "One will be enough. Target their communications infrastructure and have Psions redeploy cyber warfare assaults; get those AA guns offline again!"

Cabal; "Understood!"

Ghaul; "And give me a progress report on the cage."

Cabal; "90 percent extension!"

Ghaul; "And the Human?"

The lights in the observation deck flickered.

Cabal; "Shield is down! I repeat, shield generator is down!"

Ghaul turned away from Iago and began walking for the door, his hands trembling at his sides in feigned calmness.

Ghaul; "Track them! Where are they going now?"

Cabal; "Top deck, port side!"

The door opened before Ghaul as he passed through the threshold, the communication moving to his mask from the throne.

Ghaul; "Send two of my blood guard their way. We shall meet them there."

The door closed behind Ghaul as he walked the halls, a pair of Cabal in gold and red armor flanking him on either side. He walked up a ramp onto the top deck to see a Human and their ghost; their armor made it impossible to tell gender, and Ghaul found them to be so scrawny and their armor so haphazard he wouldn't bother to tell if they were wearing a cloak, robes or a loincloth... But, he heard the voice of their drone, hovering only a foot from their shoulder.

Drone; "... How do we come back from this?"

Ghaul spoke as soon as he stepped into the light of the storm and the fight around them.

Ghaul; "You don't."

He continued approaching, gesturing to the Traveler with his left hand as the pair looked at him.

Ghaul; "Welcome to a world... without Light."

At the moment the Human and their drone turned back to the Traveler, an orange aura encircled the sphere, and a silhouette of cyan light separated from the Human, the drone sounding faint as they spoke.

Drone; "Guardian... Something's wrong..."

The drone fell to the ground and powered off, coinciding with the Human dropping to their hands and knees. Ghaul restrained a laugh as he watched them crumple to the ground, fists still clenched at his sides as the Human clutched their drone and pulled them close. When the Human looked up to Ghaul, he intensified his glare, raising his voice.

Ghaul; "Do *not* look at me, creature!"

He then kicked them away with his right foot, knocking the weapon from their other hand as they stumbled onto their back. Ghaul continued walking to them, speaking all the while.

Ghaul; "You are weak; undisciplined. Cowering behind walls."

The Guardian attempted to stand again, Ghaul maintaning a menacing saunter to approach.

Ghaul; "You're not brave... You've merely forgotten the fear of death."

Ghaul bent down to meet the Guardians gaze once they got to their feet again.

Ghaul; "Allow me to reacquaint you."

He reared his right arm and backhanded the Guardian, throwing them all the way to the edge of the ship and knocking the drone from their hand, leaving the Guardian to silently reach for it as it plummeted to the earth below.

Ghaul; "Your kind never deserved the power you were given."

The Guardian turned around and faced Ghaul, their arms hanging hopelessly at their sides as they sat on their knees, posture weak and wobbly.

Ghaul; "I am Ghaul... And your Light?"

He pointed to the Traveler as the Guardian lifted their head to meet Ghauls gaze.

Ghaul; "... Is mine."

Ghaul lifted his left leg and kicked the Guardian from the ship, lingering and watching them fall a few seconds before turning around, hearing the Cabal officer in his ears again.

Cabal; "Dominus. The Speaker has been located... There's someone else with them. They're asking to speak to you."

Ghaul let out a sigh as he began walking for the door back inside the ship.

Ghaul; "Get transmat systems online and put them in my observation room."

When Ghaul returned to the observation room, he saw a Hive rune circle flare with green flames, instinctively reaching for his sidearm. His eyes widened to see two Humans manifest from the flames; one was an Awoken Warlock in green and black robes, her eyes shining like emeralds. The other Human was beaten and battered, a white mask over their face, laying on the ground in a heap. Ghaul raised an eyebrow and approached with apprehension, still ready to draw his pistol.

Ghaul; "... Identify yourself, *Guardian*."

The Awoken chuckled lowly as she rested her right elbow in her left palm, examining the burns from the Soulfire on the tips of her fingers.

Awoken; "Call me Herra, you oversized marshmallow. I come to you with one very simple request; grant it, and I will turn over the Speaker."

She gestured to the Human on the ground as Ghaul stood near the top of the stairs, his right foot at the top of the steps, folding his arms over his chest.

Ghaul; "... And what do you request?"

Herra mimicked Ghauls pose, a smirk growing on her face.

Herra; "All the knowledge and research on the Hive you gathered from the Dreadnaught of the Taken King."

Ghaul took a moment to ponder the requisition, head tilted towards the ground.

Herra; "Do not ask yourself if you can afford to take this risk, Dominus; ask yourself only, if you can afford *not* to take this risk."

Ghaul let out a low growl before looking back up to meet Herras gaze.

Ghaul; "A Psion will beam the information directly to you."

Herra nodded with a widening smile as a Psion entered the room behind Ghaul, pressing two fingers to the side of their head. Herra blinked rapidly as the data filled her mind, Ghaul swiftly drawing his sidearm and thumbing the safety, firing a shot at Herra.

Herra; "Lokaar!"

The Awoken then disappeared in a flurry of smoke and Soulfire, making the round explode and shatter the window of the observation deck out. Ghaul growled and lowered his weapon before turning to the Psion.

Ghaul; "...Don't just stand there, bind him! I will speak with him as soon as he's awake."

CHAPTER 1

S ix months until war

Evelyn walked across the Courtyard of the Tower away from Banshee, waving to a Frame in front of a large monitor as she made her way to a door directly across from Banshee, pushing an Omolon jug aside as she walked in. She'd glance to the front page of the stapled documents, bearing only a large Omolon logo on the front, as she walked the halls and began to see Future War Cult banners hung on the walls of the hallway, finding herself in a small room that held a Vex Gate structure, a gurney angled near vertical built into the Vex metal and concrete, connected by a large cable. The cable ran through the headrest and was situated to connect to the back of an Exos head.

In the seat was Lakshmi-2, her facial "muscles" twitching occasionally, static sparking on the exterior of the gate. Eve watched with apprehnsion as she stepped towards a collapsible table and set the papers down. She watched Lakshmi convulse for another minute or so before she gasped awake, immediately unplugging herself from the machine and stumbling down to her hands and knees. Evelyn came to her aid, resting a hand on her shoulder, her voice permated with worry.

Eve; "You alright, Lakshmi? How do you feel?"

Lakshmi, with shaky breathing, turned her head up to Evelyn and took her outstretched hand, allowing the Warlock to help her to her feet.

Lakshmi; "I'm fine, Evelyn... I've seen something terrible. The Device sets it to be six months from now."

Eves brows raised in surprise as she removed her hand from Lakshmis shoulder.

Eve; "What did you see?"

Lakshmi made broad, wild gestures as she spoke about the vision.

Lakshmi; "I saw the sky ablaze with cannon fire, banners of red, legions of soldiers bringing death to the city... You should see for yourself."

Eve held a hand to her chest, swallowing a knot in her throat.

Eve; "... Will I be ok? I've heard people go crazy after just a few *seconds*, and I've seen you in there for *hours*."

Lakshmi reached a hand up and held Eves close to her chest in a reassuring manner.

Lakshmi; "Others, yes. They were either Human or Awoken. *You* are an Exo, perfectly designed to handle the mind forking process."

Eve gave a gentle nod before wandering over to the machine, Lakshmi helping her get settled into it.

Eve; "... What will I see, generally?"

Lakshmi gently plugged the cable into the back of Evelyns head, and Eves breathing got a little heavier afterwards.

Lakshmi; "Many paths untrodden... Focus on one, or you'll be in there longer than you'd like."

Eve closed her eyes, taking deep breaths as she felt something akin to a million, million needles poking into her br ain... Not painfully, no; more like psychic acupuncture. She focused on one of the needles, allowing it to drive deeper into her metaphysical mind. When she opened her eyes, she was standing on the deck of an immense red ship, hovering over the Last City, AA guns booming from both below on the ground and from cannons on the ships top deck. She gazed down at the city before hearing a whoosh, like the igniting of a fire, seeing a pillar of Solar Light towards the center of the craft. She looked up from the column of flame to see the Traveler, glowing red and orange, light and plasma draining from outward towards the center of the apparatus surrounding it, which seemed to funnel the energy into the towering blaze. She heard a booming, deep voice from within the fire, and she flicked her wrists; they began to crackle with Arc Light as she held them up defensively.

"Fitting your Traveler would send you to face me once more."

Eve began to take slow, measured steps closer, keeping her hands raised as the flames shrank away, revealing a Cabal in white and gold armor, a large gray pack on their back that glowed with Solar Light, and their eyes briefly hissing with the plasma also.

"Look upon me-"

He stood as he spoke, gesturing broadly with his arms.

"Dominus of the Red Legion; Annihilator of suns. Razer of a thousand worlds, slayer of gods and conqueror of the Light! I, am, Ghaul!"

Eve tensed her jaw as Ghaul drew a sidearm from his thigh, leveling it with his shoulder with the barrel pointing skyward.

Ghaul; "And I have become legend."

He leapt into the air first by the fires of a jet pack, but then was enrobed in Solar Light fire and smoke, conjuring a cleaver-like blade of Solar metal alloy before hurling it at Evelyn. She managed to Ionic Blink out of the way, but she was struck by a second thrown blade, and she was jolted back into the real world with a shriek, falling from The Device, the cable still plugged into the back of her head. A few FWC members came to her aid, Lakshmi kneeling down in front of Evelyn with an arm resting across her thigh.

Lakshmi; "Now you see why I was worried, yes?"

Evelyn took in a sharp inhale as she was helped to her feet, massaging her back with a shaky exhale, her voice still exhuding concern.

Eve; "Yeah... You said this was supposed to be six months out?

Lakshmi nodded, clasping her hands in front of her waist as she stood in sync with Eve.

Lakshmi; "Yes... We've not picked up anything extrasolar on the sattelites yet, though I would not be surprised if they account of that as well... Did you happen to bring the order?"

Eve; "Uh... Yeah, right over there."

Evelyn pointed to the paperwork she'd originally brought in, still resting on the table. Lakshmi walked over and picked it up, skimming through the first couple pages before stopping at the fourth and reading it thoroughly, mumbling to herself as she read.

Lakshmi; "61 Auto rifles, 60 Scout rifles, 91 Pulse rifles, 74 Submachine guns, 80 Fusion rifles..."

She sighed and set the papers back on the table, irately tapping her foot.

Lakshmi; "Less than half of what I had hoped for... And they won't be here for a few months. We need more arms, more armor, quickly."

Eve folded her arms over her chest, avoiding mimicking Lakshmis posture.

Eve; "Can we not order more? Heck, maybe get Guardians to donate some?"

Lakshmi shook her head, as if to say no.

Lakshmi; "We have neither the Glimmer nor the reputation to be asking more of the City and its Guardians..."

She bowed her head a moment before looking at Evelyn with only her eyes, almost as if pleaing.

Lakshmi; "I understand you're an officer of the law, Evelyn... But I'm afraid we must turn to... outside dealers."

Eve raised an eyebrow, tilting her head slightly to the side.

Eve; "You know one?"

Lakshmi nodded with pursed "lips".

Lakshmi; "Indeed, I do... He operates out of the Reefs borders, so you won't have to worry about Awoken patrols. It's a lawless, tangled mess out there, but I expect you to navigate it well."

Eve nodded with a furrowed brow, letting out a quiet sigh.

Eve; "Alright... Who am I looking for?"

Lakshmi; "I only know him by name; The Spider."

CHAPTER 2

Three months until war

A City-made Hawk flies down to one of many hangars along the wall of the Last City, turning clockwise so it was facing the exit of the hangar for a quick departure. It levitated over an overhanging landing pad on the exterior of the citys borders, transmatting Evelyn out of the ship as a ramp lowered. A dozen frames began a march onto the langing pad and into the ship, weapon racks and crates in hand as they began to augment the ship. Evelyn waved to an Awoken nearby in black and white as she walked up a flight of stairs into a boot overlooking the hangar, boldly emblazoned with the FWC logo on the side. She entered the room and gave a bow to Lakshmi at the other end of the room, whom was sitting cross legged with a data pad in hand.

Eve; "Lakshmi. You said it was my turn to haul the weapons here?"

Lakshmi looked up from her tablet with a gentle smile, pulling herself from her seat to stand.

Lakshmi; "Yes, it is, Officer. Dead Orbit was kind enough to let us borrow their landing zone, so no snide comments or looks."

Eve let out a huff of amusement as she followed Lakshmi out of the booth, clasping her hands behind her back.

Eve;"Oh, don't worry about that! I always wave hello... Though, Jalaal always seems to be in a bad mood."

Lakshmi; "Dead Orbit as a whole usually is."

The two made their way out of the booth and towards the landing pad Eve originally set the ship over to find half a dozen boxes set outside the ship, open and empty. Eve wandered over to one of the larger crates and closed it, sitting on the lid whilst resting her hands in her lap.

Eve; "So, who is this Spider guy? How do you know him?"

Lakshmi let out a dry chuckle as she turned to face Eve, clasping her hands in front of her waist as the ambient Frames began to move the boxes into the ship.

Lakshmi; "I know him through a... mutual friend. I'm not at liberty to say more, but she has weapons knowledge and he has the means to make them... Not exactly, but good enough. I've never seen him in person."

Eve nodded gently, pulling herself off the final crate so the Frames could take it up the ships open ramp.

Eve; "Alright... I'll try not to offend, if he's been this helpful."

Lakshmi gave Eve a polite bow, which Eve reciprocated. She wandered up into the ship and closed up the ramp, sitting in the co-pilots seat and holding out her left hand. She spoke with a soft voice, as if to not be too disruptive.

Eve; "Nolan... Can you please take me to the coordinates Lakshmi gave?"

Nolan materialized in her palm with what could be approximated to be a scowl on his face.

Nolan; "Yeah... I got this."

He proceeded to flutter up to a small alcove in the ceiling above the pilots seat, which seemed to hold a miniaturized version of the console, which he proceeded to scan over with a cone of blue light. Outside the ship, the ramp closed up and the thrusters revved as the ship proceeded to take off for orbit, the port and starboard thrusters angling horizontal as the vessel blasted skyward. Lakshmi mumbled under her breath as she watched their contrails fade into the wind.

Lakshmi; "...And don't go to Neptune, whatever you do."-Eve and Nolan exited FTL just outside of the Reef, the cabin illuminated with the amethyst glow of spectral dust. Eve leaned forward with an open mouth smile to look at the variety of asteroids and spaceship wrecks that floated about. The ship flew through the clouds of lavender for almost half an hour before arriving at a gathering of rocks and boulders held together by Fallen designed tethers and chains, Eve eyeing what appeared to be a Fallen Ketch off to the right and painted orange and black. She looked to the left to see the ship coming to a stop at a makeshift dock made from Fallen ship parts and detritus and stone. She stood from her seat and held out a hand for Nolan, who flew down from the alcove and disappeared one he reached her hand.

Eve; "Thank you, Nolan... Really."

She heard Nolan over her comms device as she rounded the hold to the ramp, taking her Tlaloc rifle and mounting it on her back.

Nolan; "Don't mention it... I thought you were supposed to know how to fly by now."

Eve paused to speak before descending the ramp.

Eve; "... He... Never got to finish teaching me. I guess I know enough but... It'd be a rough ride."

She waited for Nolan to respond, only for about 15 seconds, before letting out a sigh and heading to the bottom of the ramp to see several Fallen standing around, spears in hand. They turned to face Eve as soon as she saw them, aiming their weapons as she drew her own, her helmet wrapping and folding over her head. One of the Shank drones spoke in English, bearing a sniper rifle like weapon on its head. Their voice was deep and heaving, as if out of breath.

Shank; "Don't attack, either of you! We can settle things diplomatically."

Evelyns eyes brightened, in lieu of widening, upon hearing a language she recognized.

Eve; "...You speak my language. Are you the Spider?"

The shank flew closer, and Eve could see a stylized spider symbol painted on the right side of the drone.

Shank; "Indeed I am...By proxy, at least. You know how these things are, it's safer where I am, especially with you Humans waving your guns around."

He let out a quiet chuckle, and the speaker hissed, as though a canister were releasing pressure on the other side.

Spider; "Best way to do business is to know what your clients are speaking. On the subject of clients... I can only assume you're the next scheduled Future War Cultist to come my way?"

Eve nodded without a word, thumbing for the safety on her rifle and slinging it onto her back once more.

Spider; "Excellent...I'll have my associates load up the ship. Our dear mutual friend has already wired me the Glimmer so...You're free to return to the ship."

Eve nodded again, folding her arms over her chest.

Eve; "If I may ask one question...Unrelated to our business."

There was a pause before Spider replied.

Spider; "Unrelated... I suppose that's fine, but make it snappy."

Eve; "...What house are you apart of?"

The Spider let out a boisterous laugh, the meaty sound of a slap heard, as if a hand slapped a knee.

Spider; "Oh, I should've seen that coming... I'm in charge of my own house, chromedome; the House of Spider. No kells, no archons... Just me and my associates, and any wayward bounty hunters and mercenaries."

Eve let out a hum of understanding, letting her arms hang down by her sides.

Eve; "Alright... Pleasure doing business with you, Spider."

Spider; "Heh, the pleasure is all mine. Enjoy your weapons... Hope they serve you well."

He laughed again as Eve turned and began walking back into the ship as Spider shouted at the nearby Eliksni to load up the ship. Evelyn whispered to Nolan as she got back into the co-pilots chair, making sure the Fallen didn't hear her.

Eve; "Nolan... As soon as they're done, drop a transmat beacon out of sight. I wanna be able to find my way back here, with reinforcements."

Nolan whispered back, despite being out of sight.

Nolan; "Ok... Why, though? He doesn't seem like a Splicer, though."

Eve; "No, but I can still keep him from doing more damage to the city. If he's willing to sell guns to us, who else is he selling to?"

Nolan; "True... But I don't think it's our business."

Eve let out a quiet, exasperated sigh and folded her arms over her chest once more.

Eve; "Well, I'm gonna make it my business."

CHAPTER 3

Evelyn walks down the stairs into the Vanguard meeting room; it was dimly lit, barely 4 in the morning. She walked past the empty desks of Shaxx and Arcite, finding only Zavala down there, writing one some documents with a pen. He sighed before looking up, giving Evelyn a respectful nod. Eve returned the greeting, keeping her hands at her sides as she spoke.

Eve; "Commander... What are you doing up so early?"

Zavala let out an amused huff, glancing to the paperwork in front of him.

Zavala; "I couldn't sleep, truth be told. So I decided to get more work done... How's work with the cult treating you, officer?"

Evelyn clasped her hands behind her back as she approached the table, standing at the opposite position of where Cayde would be.

Eve; "I just got back from the Reef, actually... I wanted to request authorization for a strike-grade operation."

He raised an eyebrow, setting down the pen as he planted his hands flat against the table.

Zavala; "A target in the Reef? Unless it's one of our own in need of rescue... I can't authorize that."

Eve leaned forward, putting a hand on the table in the same manner as Zavala.

Eve; "He's a Fallen peddling arms out there, I think that's worth going after."

Zavala shook his head with a sigh, his head bowed. He raised it to make eye contact with Evelyn, resting a hand over top hers.

Zavala; "Believe me, Evelyn, I would love nothing more than to put another Fallen in the ground... But if they're in the Reef, that's Mara Sovs problem. If you want to deal with it, you talk to her. We have no jurisdiction there."

Eves jaw tensed a moment before she pulled away, standing upright.

Zavala; "I know you're angry at our enemies, after what they've taken from you... They've taken from all of us. We have to remember what's important, and prioritize that."

She nodded before letting out a sigh, leaving the meeting room. Zavala watched her leave, eyes lingering on her footsteps and her bowed head before picking up his pen and continuing with the paperwork.------In orbit of Pluto, a sterile white space station hung over the surface, immobile and powerless. All around it, scores of red spacecraft appeared, as if the stars were bleeding. Above the station, an immense metal structure like a sideways H appeared, and many more ships emerged between the "wings" to escort it. Zooming in on one would we see a Cabal in white, gold and red armor, his arms folded over his chest as he stood in front of a viewscreen; Ghaul himself. He spoke to no one in particular, a light on his throne behind him flashing red.

Ghaul; "Navigator, what's the nearest concentration of Light apart from Earth?"

A voice came through the speaker on the chair and through unseen speakers in the corners of the room. Behind that, the door to the room opened to a Cabal in black and red armor, tanks of a viscous purple fluid on their back and a flamethrower-type weapon on their hip like a sidearm. He knelt as soon as he reached the top of the stairs, listening to the conversation.

Navigator; "Sensing... Closest concentration is near one of the gas giants. The largest gas giant, actually... Third largest of the moons, and one of the closest that are still roughly spherical. Sulfur heavy, volcanically active... And brimming with Light signatures."

Ghaul let out an amused grunt, his face creasing with a smirk under his mask.

Ghaul; "Prepare a detachment of ships to go there and begin excavations; We will not leave a single drop for the inhabitants of this system."

Navigator; "Aye, sir."

The newly arrived Cabal cleared their throat to get Ghauls attention, to which they turned around, letting his arms hang at his sides.

Ghaul; "Ca'uor... That is your name, is it not?"

He stood at attention.

Ca'uor; "Yes, Dominus. I came to request permission to lead the mining expedition to the moon."

Ghaul began to walk closer. Inside his helmet, Ca'uors breathing got heavier out of anxiety, but he stood his ground.

Ghaul; "You wish to prove yourself worthy of a promotion... Do you, Ca'uor?"

Ca'uor gave a stiff nod before responding.

Ca'uor; "Yes, Dominus. I would hope to be your most useful soldier."

Ghaul emitted another grunt of amusement, leaning down so he was at eye level with Ca'uor.

Ghaul; "Need I remind you that those before Acrius burned their hands on the sun when they attempted to claim it? Do not reach for power so greedily, Val."

Ca'uor nodded again, taking in a deep breath.

Ca'uor; "I understand, Dominus. I will temper my ambition s... But my loyalties to you are immutable."

Ghaul nodded before turning away, walking back to the viewscreen.

Ghaul; "I would hope so..."

He sighed before looking over his shoulder to Ca'uor.

Ghaul; "Take a couple cruisers to the moon, and do not break active camouflage until the Traveler is ours. Limit your explorations to areas not actively being patrolled, do *not* engage the enemy until I say so."Ca'uor bowed before speaking.

Ca'uor; "The Light is yours, Dominus."

He then promptly turned around and departed the room, leaving Ghaul alone to watch the fleet move towards the inner system.

Chapter 4

One week until war

Evelyns ship flies overhead towards a clearing in the Cosmodrome, passing through clouds of rising smoke and embers. On the ground, half a dozen Guardians wielded Solar Light in their hands in the form of blades, guns, hammers or gouts of flame, sublimating the leftover SIVA cables and wires that ran through the landscape and ruins of buildings.

Evelyn herself was on the ground, hands brimming with Solar flame as she watched a SIVA node fall apart in a bonfire like a yule log. The sun was beginning to peek through the clouds above her, and the snow was beginning to melt, gradually. She took in deep breaths, exhaling slowly as the memory of her fight with Rahndel ran through her mind; the disgusting squelch as her Dawnblade penetrated his center mass, the smell of burning flesh as she enflamed the sword, the cries of pain and agony as he was burned alive-

She was pulled from her thoughts by a hand being gingerly rested on her shoulder. She straightened her posture and turned to look at who it was; Cayde, a soft smile on his face.

Cayde; "Hey... You doin' ok, kiddo?"

Eve nodded gently as she looked away, turning back to the blaze.

Eve; "Yeah... Just, thinking."

Cayde playfully pushed Eves shoulder, letting out a chuckle.

Cayde; "You Warlocks do too much of that thinking stuff. Be more like Thagomizer over there; not a single synapse has fired under that helmet in 20 years."

He turned back to point at a Titan in vibrant lavender armor, a pair of horns protruding from each pauldron. Cayde shouted to them in the distance, a hand held perpendicular to his mouth.

Cayde; "Ain't that right, Thag?!"

The Titan flexed their biceps with a gravelly, roaring voice.

Thag; "THAAAAG!"

Thag proceeded to turn around and headbutt a burning SIVA cable with his helmet, producing a metal clunk, causing Eve to chuckle a little. Cayde patted Eve on the shoulder, looking back to the burning SIVA node.

Cayde; "We can take it from here, Officer; you've had a rough... Hell, a rough year, let alone few months. Take a week off, take care of yourself."

Eve turned her head downward slightly, letting out a quiet sigh.

Eve; "But...There's still a lot of work to do...Someone needs to do all that paperwork that Wyrm wasn't able to finish, and there's more every day-"

She's cut off by Cayde holding a straight finger to her "lips".

Cayde; "Look, I skimp out on the paperwork all the time; it's not gonna kill Ikora if it's a little late. Besides, I believe you can't do your work properly if you don't take care of yourself!"

Eve grew a slight smirk on her face.

Eve; "Sneaking out to the casino counts as taking care of yourself?"

Cayde furrowed his brow a little, but his tone was still a blend of mischevious and genuine.

Cayde; "Don't change the subject on me now; Go back to the city, tell Ikora you want at least a week off. The day's coming up... I know I wouldn't wanna work on a day like that."

Eve took a deep breath before responding in a hushed voice.

Eve; "Alright... Thank you, Cayde."

Cayde patted her shoulder with a smile as she walked over to her ship, the ramp lowering the closer she got.

Cayde; "No problem. Hey, I'll buy you a drink when I'm done here, eh?"

Eve stopped halfway up the ramp before turning back to Cayde, a smile creeping up on her faceplate.

Eve; "... Maybe. We'll see how I'm feeling."

Cayde shrugged, pulling his revolver from his hip and igniting it in Solar Light.

Cayde; "Alright, more for me if you decide to stay home!"-In orbit of Io, seven Red Legion cruisers descend through the atmosphere, their hulls burning white hot. One of them came to hover over an immense cradle erected in a sinkhole. A hangar opens at the underbelly and releases a Harvester dropship, flying down towards the cradles center. Upon reaching the center, the sides of the Harvester opened up and released eight Legionaries, donned in red armor with retractable blades on their left arms, their fingers and thumbs replaced with cybernetics. A platform lowered underneath the Harvester to reveal Ca'uor, staring ahead at what lay at the center of the cradle.

At the center was an immense tree of silvery white bark, its branches swirling and growing into a spherical shape. One of the Legionaries came to walk alongside Ca'uor as he began making his way to the tree. He turned his eyes to the Legionary as his helmet retracted and folded around his neck.

Ca'uor; "The Light was strongest here?"

The Legionary nodded, their facial expressions concealed by their helmet.

Legionary; "Yes, sir: There's one other in the system that we're aware of, on the fourth planet. We assume it's the mark left from planetary engineering."

Once at one of the roots, Ca'uor knelt down to look more closely at it, narrowing his eyes.

Ca'uor; "Interesting... See what your science team can do with a sample, hmm?"

He said this as he reached down to grip the root and pull a piece off.-As soon as he laid his hands on it, his vision turned white and he saw himself aboard an opulent vessel, stomping up a flight of stairs to stand in front of a Cabal automaton, golden in color with red eyes and a cannon on its right arm. He heard his own voice speak to the machine as the vision played out.

Ca'uor; "...This system belongs to the Cabal now. We never needed you, Calus... if only to see how not to have our empire run. *I* will be the new Emperor, and *you* will be lost to the annals of time. How does that sound?"

The automaton shook its head in disappointment, its left hand subtly charging with violet psychic energy.

Calus; "You no longer amuse me, Ca'uor..."

Calus then turned to look at the door onto the bridge of the ship, which was beginning to open.

Calus; "My more accomodating guests have arrived to usher you out."

Ca'uor looked to the opening door as well, spotting half a dozen Humans in armor run through the door. He swung a left hook at the Cabal machine, then backhanded the Calus automaton onto its back. He activated his jump pack and leapt into the air, activating it again once he was overhead of the Guardians, his vision flashing once more.-Ca'uor stood and took a couple steps back, holding a hand to his head, groaning quietly.

Legionary; "Val, are you well?"

Ca'uor waved a hand in dismissal, taking in a deep breath as he massaged his glabella.

Ca'uor; "I'll live... We will *not* excavate here. We will extract the Light further West, near the Human bunker."

The Legionary nodded, saluting Ca'uor by pounding a fist to his chest.

Legionary; "By your command... But, what of the tree?"

Ca'uor swung his arm back to his side with a grunt.

Ca'uor; "Leave it... This is sacred ground."

CHAPTER 5

The rain wracked the roof of the Tower hangar like nails driving down against a wooden board, practically indistinguishable from a bucket of water being poured from above. Eve, a tense expression on her faceplate, stood under the roof with her arms folded over her chest, watching the rain come down before the morning light. She had her scout rifle and fusion rifle on her back, a belt-fed machine gun resting on a table behind her, Future War Cult purple. Soon, she was approached by Nolan from behind, a newspaper roll stuck between pieces of his shell and bound with a rubber band. He watched the rain with her with a sigh before speaking.

Nolan; "... Why be up here? You know your week off starts tomorrow, right? You could've given yourself an extra day."

Eve glanced to Nolan, taking a deep breath before speaking, her brow furrowing slightly.

Eve; "I've got a job to do, Nolan... I'm not gonna abandon it just because I'm uncomfortable."

Nolan turned to Eve, adjusting the newspaper betwixt his shell pieces.

Nolan; "You think that's what Wyrm would've wanted?"

Eve finally locked gaze with Nolan, a frown on her face.

Eve; "How could you know what he wanted? You hardly talked to him, you hardly talk to me! You just want to go down to the Core to gossip with that tabloid journalist!"

Nolans eye closed halfway, mimicking the expression of unamusement.

Nolan; "Alright, Sherlock, you got me there. Am I wrong to want to do a little something for myself?"

Eve let out a frustrated sigh as she fully turned to face him.

Eve; "Y'know what? If you don't care, go on ahead without me! I'm not going on patrol today, so I don't need you."

Nolans voice took on an almost triumphant tone, with just a touch of curiosity.

Nolan; "That makes two of us... But why did it take you so long to figure that out?"

Eves eyes glowed brighter, and she leaned in closer to Nolan, taking on a more aggressive stance, not quite raising her voice.

Eve; "You think... You can just be selfish today? On the day Wyrm and Jade were murdered?"

Nolan rolled his cyclopic eye before speaking.

Nolan; "I got news for you, kid; There's a million Guardians and Ghosts out there just like them, they weren't anything special."

Eve lunged forward and grabbed Nolan by the core, shouting at him as she held him, making him drop the newspaper.

Eve; "**THEY WERE SPECIAL TO ME!**"

Nolan froze with a wide eye, and Evelyn slowly let go of him when she realized what she was doing, bringing her hands to her sides, her voice small now.

Eve; "...Just go. You can meet me back in the ship."

Eve sighed as Nolan levitated down and pinched the newspaper between his shell pieces again before floating down from the Tower, down to the city below. With shaky breathing, she rested her hands on her hips and walked further inwards towards the security gate. She sat on the crate that held her machine gun, massaging her face a moment before leaning over to pick up a datapad. She tapped a couple icons to begin calling Nolan, the "phone" ringing for several seconds before an automated message was heard.

"I'm sorry, service is not available at this time."

She frowned and tapped the tablet a couple times before she heard a noise coming from the direction of the city. She perked her head up as she recognized it; an air raid siren. She jumped to her feet just before explosions began rocking the Tower, sending debris crumbling on top of her. The weight of the stone and concrete knocked her to her back, threatening to crush her chest and legs. She struggled to push it off her, hyperventilating and near panicking as she heard cannon fire and missiles fly overhead. She looked at her hands, pushing against the detritus and keeping her from being crushed. She closed her eyes and took a deep breath, dark violet plasma beginning to hiss from her eyes.

With a roar, her body was enrobed in Void Light and she released a shockwave of plasma, disintigrating the rubble and freeing herself. When she got up, she glowered when she saw her machine gun was half-destroyed; missing most of the barrel and the belt box spilling its bullets, still burning with Void plasma. With a sigh, she drew her Susanoo fusion rifle and ran out into the open, seeing a fleet of crimson ships fly overhead, one of them opening up like a flower into a six pointed shape, flying towards the Traveler. Eves eyes widened when she heard the voice of Zavala behind her, up near the entrance to Travelers Walk, and she turned to look his way.

Zavala; "This is Commander Zavala; Civillians, report to evac points. Guardians, rendezvous in the plaza, our city will *not* fall!"

She could see he was holding a Nadir assault rifle painted in the Vanguards usual blue and orange, ushering Banshee and several other civillians out to a few Hawks landed on the concrete out back. Eve ran towards Zavala and the civillians as he cocked back the bolt of his weapon.

Eve; "Commander! What do you want me to do?"

Zavala briefly smiled upon seeing Evelyn, thumbing the safety on his rifle.

Zavala; "Officer, good to see you. The Cabal are besieging the city, and we've gotten a steady stream of evac ships heading for Mercury... Here's hoping Vance and his little cult is accepting refugees."

He gestured to the ships behind him.

Zavala; "This is the last of the civillians in the Tower. Once they're away, I want you back out here for your next target."

Eve saluted the Commander, and Zavala returned the gesture.

Eve; "They won't even scratch the paint, sir."

She ran back towards the ships, thumbing the safety on her fusion rifle. She gave a wave to Banshee before she heard a crack, like lightning, and she mumbled to herself as she scanned the skies.

Eve; "Nolan, where are you...?"

The Tower rumbled as it was hit by a large black sphere with indentations, hitting the concrete just above the entry to the Walk, putting debris between the Commander and herself. The sphere dislodged after a second or two, hitting the ground and expanding a quarter of its size, the area between its indentations glowing orange-white hot. The hard black shell dissolved, revealing an evaporating shell of oil underneath, which gave way to a trio of Cabal Legionaries, wearing red armor and holding shotguns with barrels that glowed blue with electricity. Eve glanced back to the ships as she leveled her rifle.

Pulling the trigger down, a flurry of Solar flames gathered at the end of the barrel before seven pellets were let loose, striking one of the Legionaries and incinerating them. The other two continued their march forward, firing on Evelyn and occasionally striking the ships behind her as they took off. She fired again, disintegrating another Legionary, taking a couple steps back as the ship behind her took off, leaving one more. The final Legionary got close enough that they moved their left arm off their weapon, a blade extending from a device on their forearm.

They took a swing at Evelyn, and she instinctively holds up her weapon to protect herself. The fusion rifle is cleaved in twain, and Eve growls before throwing the halves away, delivering a punch to the Cabals gut... But not fazing them. The Cabal emitted a facsimile of a laugh as it backhanded her away, knocking her to her back. With a groan, she got up and flicked her wrist, gathering Arc Light before holding out an open hand, lightning streaming out and electrocuting the Legionary, making them crumple to the ground. She breathed heavily as the static dissipated from her arm, looking at the armor of the Cabal. She then got a call from Cayde, heard through the comms device on her wrist.

Cayde; "Hey, kiddo, you still with us?"

Eve nodded before responding.

Eve; "I'm here, Cayde. Where are you?"

Caydes call started to get staticky, and his ship passed overhead.

Cayde; "I uh... Got some precious, one-eyed cargo that can read minds, can you get their rescue party off my tail?"

Eve blinked a couple times as she processed what he said.

Eve; "You kidnapped a Psion?! Who are they sending after you?!"

The Tower rumbled as a Cabal carrier flew overhead, and Cayde sheepishly replied through static.

Cayde; "Um... Definitely more than two guys."

Eve let out a huff as she ignited her frame in Solar Light.

Eve; "I'll do what I can."

She faced her palms to the ground, spewing flames from her hands, ankles and back in the form of wings, taking flight towards the warship. She turned her eyes towards the Traveler and the Last City... Seeing the immense ship wrap its metal tendrils around the Traveler. She whispered to herself, barely able to hear herself between the rush of wind and roar of flames.

Eve; "Stay safe, Nolan..."

She turned back to the carrier, fast approaching it as it ascends through the atmosphere. Once Eve was a quarter of the way over top of the ship, she dove down and crashed into the hull with an explosion of Solar flames and smoke. She landed on her face, slowly standing with heavy breathing, her movements slowed from exhaustion. She looked around to see she was in a cargo hold of some kind, a large structure with antennae. She leaned against it before reaching behind herself for her scout rifle... But it wasn't there. She patted her back with both hands before looking up to the hole she entered in, letting out a frustrated groan.

Before she could move for the door, a light blue silhouette separated from her, and weakness overcame her even more than before. She held up a hand and watched as Void Light attempted to make a sphere in her hands... But it dissolved before it could properly manifest. She dropped to one knee, breathing heavily and clutching a hand to her chest before falling to her back, eyes struggling to stay open.

The cargo hold faded around her as she caught sight of a small, vaporous bird taking flight, going over a pale yellow crater that held the Traveler. She saw water near the cradle, and could see people that had drowned in the depths of the water. She also saw pyramids diving into the water, followed by an immense ship or space station consuming a planet. Images of lightning in the shape of a quarterstaff, fire in the shape of a sword and Void plasma in the shape of a shield flashed in her mind as she eyed the hawk one last time, flying towards a large hunk of the Traveler that was embedded in the Earth.

By the time the vision faded, she opened her eyes again to see she was on the ground of some kind of alien planet with green skies and red trees, no longer inside the Cabal carrier. The carrier was now overhead, the structure she was next to now deployed on the ground. She struggled to get up, letting out a shout of pain before falling over again. With a clenched jaw, she looked to her feet to see the her legs were snapped from the knees down, hanging on by scant few cables and wires. Her fists clenched and dug up the ground beneath her as she winced away in pain, fading into unconsciousness bit by bit. The last thing she remembered hearing was insect-like chittering, and the sheathing of swords.

Chapter 6

Evelyn slowly opened her eyes, head pounding and breathing shallow as she slowly regained her senses. She attempted to rub her face... But she couldn't move her hands out from her sides; they were bound by the wrist. She gasped and looked up, finding her mouth was also gagged with some kind of cloth. She was in a natural cave of some kind, the entrance visible from where she was sat. She looked down to see her legs were still broken, everything from the knees down removed and the fluid cables cauterized. She heard a voice, speaking English, but slightly raspy and muffled, as though speaking through a mask.

"I told you we can't trust them! Now we're gonna have to go elsewhere!"

Eve turned to see a pair of Fallen standing off to the side, both in purple House regalia; a Vandal and a Captain. The Captain held an Arc spear, which was impaled through the back of a House Winter Dreg on the ground, while the Vandal was sat on a rock with a pair of Shock Pistols holstered under her upper arms. The Captain spoke as she removed the spear from the Dreg, wiping the pale blue blood from the blade on her loincloth.

Captain; "It doesn't matter now... Other crews will be here soon, hearing the scuffle. We'll have to find another hole to hide out in until we can get a new Pike... A Skiff, preferably."

The Vandal spoke as Eve watched them, making sure her eyes were dim, as to not draw attention to herself.

Vandal; "But why bother getting a Skiff if we're not leaving Nessus?"

Eves couldn't help but look surprised upon the mention of the planetoids name, accidentally mumbling through the gag over her mouth.

Eve; "Mm-mmph?!"

She froze as both of the Fallen turned to look at her, the Captain flourishing the spear before pointing it squarely at Eve, making her lean back into the corner. The Vandal jumped to her feet and held out a hand in front of the Captain, her tone sounding distressed.

Vandal; "Mother, please! We found her without her little servitor and with broken legs, she's not a threat!"

Eve squirmed in place, her breathing picking up and getting heavier, more frantic.

Captain; "You've seen what they can do, even without weapons, they're not defenseless!"

The Vandal moved between her mother and Eve, the latter closing her eyes as she felt the tingling static from the tip of the spear, whimpering quietly as her jaw was barely able to quiver due to the cloth over her mouth.

Vandal; "Just look at her, damnit! She'd be begging if she could speak! Please, for once, listen to me!"

The Captain looked between the Vandal and the trembling Exo, letting out a frustrated sigh before lowering the spear.

Captain; "Fine… You talk to her, though. I'm gonna pack everything up."

The Vandal nodded before approaching Evelyn, whom partially opened her eyes, but was still on the verge of tears and quietly whimpering. The Vandal made a shushing sound to calm Evelyn before whispering, straddling her lap and cupping her face with her upper hands.

Vandal; "Shh… It's ok. I'm not going to hurt you, ok?"

Eve blinked rapidly at how close the Fallen was, and how… tender, her actions were. She nodded gently in response, her breathing slowing down. She refrained from leaning into the Fallens touch… As much as she wanted to enjoy it. "At least they're not Devils", she thought to herself.

Vandal; "I know Humans and Eliksni don't have the best relations, but I need you trust me, yeah?"

"Eliksni? That's what they call themselves?", she pondered, eyes peering down at the Vandals hands on her cheeks. Her three fingers were warm and gentle, the nails ground down so they weren't sharp points. She met the Vandals eyes again before nodding once more.

Vandal; "Ok... I'm gonna take off the straps on your face, and I want you to tell me how you got here, alright?"

Eve took a deep breath before responding one last time with a nod. The Vandal retuned the nod and reached behind Eves head, undoing the knot and removing the cloth gag, tying the straps around her right ankle afterwards. Evelyn flexed her jaw around before taking another slow, deep breath before the Vandal spoke quietly once more.

Vandal; "Better?"

Eve barely nodded, squirming a little under the Vandal as she whispered in reply.

Eve; "Yeah, but... You can get off my lap now."

The Vandal let out a nervous chuckle before standing, clasping her lower hands behind her back.

Vandal; "Heh... Sorry. I just... Would've hated to see you panic."

The Captain returned soon after, carrying a large net with supplies and containers in it.

Captain; "Are you ready to go?"

The Vandal looked back to the Captain, her brow furrowing.

Vandal; "*You*? She's coming with us, she'll die out here."

The Captain, set down the net next to the Vandal, her voice stern.

Captain; "She can use her Light, she'll be fine."

The Vandal stood, placing her upper hands on her hips.

Vandal; "Don't you think if she *could* use her powers, she'd have blown us up by now?"

The Captain pondered for a moment, all four eyes darting between the two before letting out a sigh, picking the net back up and slinging it over her shoulder.

Captain; "Fine... But *you're* carrying her, she's your responsibility."

The Vandal nodded before removing more straps from around her abdomen and arms.

Vandal; "Yes, mother."

The Vandal proceeded to tie the cloth strips togeher, and them wrapped them around Eve, hoisting the Exo up onto her back, much to Eves mix of discomfort and awkwardness. Eve spoke as the Vandal followed the Captain out of the cave, looking out over a large crimson canopy, occasionally pierced by a sea green sky.

Vandal; "You never answered my questions."

Evelyn looked up to the sky as she was carried, tensing her jaw before speaking.

Eve; "I'm uh... Evelyn-7, Security Officer for the Tower. The Cabal sent a legion to attack the Last City... They captured the Traveler. Whatever they did to it cut off the Light, and I can't use my powers. I got here because I followed one of the Vanguard leaders here after they captured a Psion. I boarded one of their ships, I lost the Light, I barely woke up on the ground next to a listening post with my legs broken... And now I'm here."

The Vandal only let out a hum in acknowledgement, and Eve sighed quietly as she watched the Vandal march behind the Captain, squirming a little and trying to free her arms to no avail.

Eve; "So, my turn... Who are you, and what happened to the rest of my legs?"

The Vandal adjusted the harness that kept Eve on her back with a grunt.

Vandal; "Try not to move too much... I'm Netrasiik, and that's my mother, Krosis."

The Captain glanced back with a huff, a small cloud of pale blue gas trailing out of her Ether mask before she returned her eyes to the road.

Netra; "Mother used the broken parts of your legs to make armor for our Shank; he scouts out new places for us to stay."

Eve raised an eyebrow, craning her neck forward a little so she was able to meet Netras eyes.

Eve; "... He?"

Netra let out a quiet giggle, briefly kneeling down to pick a red flower from the soil along the path.

Netra; "Yeah! We call him Shar, which means brave in our tongue."

Netra eventually stopped alongside Krosis when they reached a sheer cliff, which ovelooked massive drills of dark gray and red metal, Cabal warships looming overhead as they excavated the blocky terrain.

Netra; "Are... Those the same Cabal that attacked the city?"

Eve took in a sharp inhale as she looked out over the landscape.

Eve; "Yeah... This must be a small contingent."

Krosis let out harsh sigh before turning around, preparing to walk the other way.

Krosis; "We'll have to go towards the Odus'ack, then. I hope you don't have to stop and eat, Evelyn; it's about a days walk."

Eve lightly shrugged her shoulders as Netra turned to follow Krosis.

Eve; "I'll be ok for a day... Can I be untied when we get there, though?"

Krosis turned back to Eve, her expression unchanging.

Krosis; "... We'll see."

CHAPTER 7

In the atmosphere of Nessus, a dozen Cabal warships entered orbit, along with half a dozen carriers. The carriers flew lower to the ground, deploying sections of large excavation towers that had arms of spinning drills, rotating clockwise around the tower. Aboard one of the ships, Val Ca'uor paces back and forth on the bridge, hands gently swaying at his sides. One of the Psions standing near a console turned to look at Val Ca'uor, his eye following him as he paced. Said Psions voice could only be heard in the minds of those nearby; they did not speak audibly.

Psion; "Val, I sense anxiety within you. Is this in regards to the Io excavation team?"

Ca'uor took in a deep breath, speaking through a sigh.

Ca'uor; "Indeed, Cyrax... I much prefer to be present during such an operation, but... The vision the tree gave me showed the former Emperors vessel in orbit of this excuse of a planet. They've yet to report back in seven micro-rotations..."

One of the monitors began buzzing, a green light flashing on the upper right corner of the screen. Ca'uor grunted as he looked at the screen, stomping over to it and tapping the button.

Ca'uor; "Ice Reaper division, what's your status? You've been radio silent for far too long! Do you read me, Lurg?!"

The Cabal replying sounded hushed and frantic, her microphone rumbling through heavy breathing and the rustling of armor.

Lurg; "I read you, Val. My division is almost completely eliminated, we were assaulted by Taken once we found the pocket of Light."

Ca'uor let out a sigh as he leaned a hand against the console, furrowing his brow.

Ca'uor; "Did you save any, at least?"

Lurg let out an exasperated sigh as the clank of armored boots against metal crept into the background, as though she were walking on a metal ramp.

Lurg; "As much as our holds could contain, what with all that reverse-engineered Hive tech... But there's so much, it's spilling into the atmosphere. We're regrouping with Vurst on the Almighty after delivering the Light to the Immortals capacitors."

Ca'uor nodded with grit teeth, responding after a moment.

Ca'uor; "Hmm... Do not regroup with Vurst, I'll need you at Nessus. I'm expecting stiff resistance there. Do you need the coordinates?"

Lurg mumbled under her breath, frustration lacing her tone.

Lurg; "*Blow me.*"

Ca'uor narrowed his eyes as he leaned in close to the speaker of the console.

Ca'uor; "What was that, Corporal?"

Lurg stuttered a moment before replying properly.

Lurg; "Uh, show me! Show me the coordinates and we'll be there forthwith."

Ca'uor nods and prepares to end the communication.

Ca'uor; "Expect that soon, then."

As soon as the call ended, Cyrax turned to Ca'uor, their meager lips barely contorting to express concern.

Cyrax; "Val, I've just received word from Firebase Hades: Thumos has been assassinated on his carrier."

Ca'uor whipped around to look at Cyrax, the fingertips of his glove scratching across the metal of the console in frustration.

Ca'uor; "What?! How?!"

Cyrax glanced to the monitor in front of him before turning back to Ca'uor and "speaking".

Cyrax; "The Humans seem to have found a Guardian that still wields the Light. They've also begun coordinating guerrilla offensives on the moon of Titan, as well as Earth. It's logical to assume they would make their way to Io as well."

Ca'uor snarled and approached Cyrax to get a better look at his monitor, glancing out of the bridge viewport to see a pair of Cabal ships entering atmosphere with his fleet.

Ca'uor; "What has Ghaul done about this?"

Cyrax kept his hands at his sides as he turned to look up at Ca'uor.

Cyrax; "To my knowledge, nothing. He does not want to be disturbed while he interrogates this "Speaker". Even Consul Iago has not made any attempt to inform him of the current situation."

Ca'uor clenched his fists at his sides for a moment before sharply exhaling.

Ca'uor; "If our new Emperor is going to indulge in his own obsessions, then I will indulge myself as well."

He turned back the the main bridge console, broadly gesturing to the bridge crew, Cyrax included.

Ca'uor; "Scour the planetoid for the most powerful Vex signature you can find! We'll use the technology to augment our weapons when the deposed Emperor makes his return!"

Meanwhile, on the ground, a tenth drill was deployed into the Nessusian soil and rock, drilling it away with brutal efficiency. Under one of the drills stood a large Vex mind, marble white chassis with a solid white eye and a left hand replaced with some kind of dual-pronged apparatus. The machine turned its gaze towards where it percieved one of the drills, and sent out a signal all throughout the cavern, calling upon Vex Goblins, Hobgoblins, Harpys and Minotaurs to defend its position. They appeared from elsewhen onto the drill platforms, catching the crews off guard, but they managed to shoot them down.

Ca'uor watched from the safety of his ship... Or so he thought. A haze of pale blue particulates filled the bridge, followed by the sudden appearance of Goblins and Harpys, opening fire on the bridge crew immediately. Ca'uor growled and smacked a button on his breastplate, projecting a shield of Void plasma around himself, Cyrax taking cover behind the captains seat. Ca'uors helmet wrapped and folded around his head as he drew his magma launcher, firing a stream of burning chemicals at the machines and melting them to scrap. Cyrax put a pair of fingers to the side of his head as a wave of Void Plasma ran out from his body. Once it reached the final Minotaur, the wave expanded into a circular influence and launched the plasma upwards, slamming the hulking automaton into the ceiling, falling back to the ground with a tremendous crash.

Once all the Vex were dead, Cyrax used another pulse of telekinetic Void power to push a button on his original monitor, and the shields were raised, indicated by a pattern of orange trapezoids fading in just outside of the viewport.

Cyrax; "Shields up, we should not expect any further incursions."

Ca'uor let out a sigh and lowered his weapon, holstering it on his hip as his helmet retracted.

Ca'uor; "Let's hope not... We'll get that Vex mind, one way or another."

CHAPTER 8

K rosis and Netra exit a cave on Nessus composed from the wreckage of a Human-made ship, Evelyn still strapped on Netras back. Eve looked around, subtly shrugging her shoulders, one after the other, still fruitlessly trying to free her arms with a sigh.

Eve; "This looks like... One of the colony ships in the Cosmodrome. How'd it end up here? I didn't think any of them launched."

Krosis glanced back to the pair, using her Arc spear like a walking stick as they descended a metal grate onto the soil below, still carrying the net of supplies on her back.

Krosis; "It's been here for quite a while, ever since we got here... I don't know what they made these ships out of, but there's still fires burning in some parts, even after hundreds of years."

Eve narrowed her eyes in confusion as they approached an open crate that seemed to lead down into another, natural cave. They went down, past some debris and more open containers before reaching a makeshift encampment, the gentle hum of electronics heard overhead. Netra glanced back to Evelyn, her mandibles subtly shifting to mimic a smile.

Netra; "We'll settle down here for now, see if we can get a Servitor salvaged together, and we can figure out our next move from there..."

Netra paused and looked away from Eve as she pondered, then looked back to Eve.

Netra; "You don't need Ether... Do you need food or water like a normal Human?"

Eve shook her head no, letting out a small chuckle as she examined the ceiling, spotting a kind of power conduit overhead that's still sparking with electricity.

Eve; "Heh... No, I don't *need* it, but it'd sure be nice. Maybe you guys can show me how to fix this tech with some Fallen techniques."

Netra grimaced under her rebreater as Krosis looked over her shoulder at Eve, brow furrowed. She took a deep breath before speaking, sounding as though she spoke through gritted teeth.

Krosis; "... I say this with great restraint; We are *not* Fallen. That is the name Humans have given us. We are called Eliksni."

Krosis turned to fully face Eve and Netra, a puff of pale blue gas coming out of either side of her rebreather.

Krosis; "If you're going to stay with me and my daughter, I *politely* request you respect that."

Eve nodded with a tense jaw; Netra could feel the Exos breathing get a little shaky out of fear.

Eve; "... Yes, ma'am."

Krosis let out a sigh and set down the net when they reached a solar panel embedded flat into the ground; part of a ramp that led up to some kind of workspace.

Krosis; "Netrasiik, please see about getting power redirected to one of the consoles here and... I'll get the Servitor core fixed up."

She narrowed her eyes in thought before grumbling in her native tongue, gesturing to Evelyn.

Krosis; "And... Untie her. If she's going to be with us, she may as well help any way she can."

Netra began to undo the harness that kept Eve on her back, trying to restrain the elation in her voice.

Netra; "Yes, mother."

Netra set Eve down on the ground gently, going around her to unbind her arms. Once unbound, Netra wrapped the straps around her arms, legs and abdomen, letting out a quiet chuckle.

Netra; "I understand why my mother was worried about you; she was there when the Saint went on his rampage on our house on Mercury."

Eve brought her hands in front of herself, massaging her wrists once free, glancing to Netra as she spoke.

Eve; "The Saint? As in Saint-14?"

Netra nodded, crouching down alongside Eve.

Netra; "That's what you call it? Uh, yes, I suppose... But, my mother; she's seen the worst of what Guardians can do, but... I still hope that, one day, I can see the best of what they can do."

Eve nodded with a sigh, looking down at her severed legs.

Eve; "I'd... love that, believe me. But... we Guardians have lost a lot to the Fa-... Eliksni. Everyone knows someone that was either killed or knows someone else that was killed by Eliksni. I lost someone close to me, too..."

She looked to Netra, her expression grim somewhat.

Eve; "It's... Definitely gonna take some time, some getting used to."

Netra nodded softly, climbing up onto one of the consoles after a moment, unplugging a cable from one of the overhead conduits before climbing down to find a place to plug it into the console. Eve watched with a curious expression, turning herself around and propping herself up with her hands on the floor just behind her.

Eve; "So... What house were you two part of? I don't know any house that was on Mercury."

Netra spoke as she struggled to get the console turned on, the plug sparking occasionally.

Netra; "House Rain is what it was called... Though, we've been hearing some refer to it as House Dusk as of late. It'll always be House Rain to me and mother."

With a frustrated sigh, she jiggled the power cable with both right hands, and the monitor for the console eventually turned on with a buzz. Netra chuckled and stood as Eve reached up to the keyboard.

Eve; "I'm gonna see if I can get in contact with the Vanguard... See if they can send someone to pick me up."

As Eve tapped in commands into the computer, Netra came to Eves side, crouching down so she was near eye level with the Exo.

Netra; "... Are they still there? You said they attacked the City, and the Light is gone. They wouldn't still be there, would they?"

Evelyn simply shrugged her shoulders, struggling to stay steady on the cauterized stumps of her legs.

Eve; "Won't know unless I try... Can you please keep me steady? Hard to stand without legs."

Netra nodded, taking hold of Eve by her waist from behind with her lower arms, making Eve swallow hard upon feeling the hands near her posterior.

Eve; "... Thank you."

The speakers hissed to life, followed by the voice of Zavala overhead as Eve tuned the computer to broadband comms.

Zavala; "Guardians; the City is lost... If there is any Light left in the system, we rally on Titan. Be brave."

Evelyn turned back to Netra and turned down the volume, the message going on a loop in the background.

Eve; "You happen to know what's on Titan?"

Netras expression turned grim as Eve allowed herself to sit back down.

Netra; "Titan... Moon of one of the gas giants, yeah? Last I heard, it was overrun with Hive from the Dreadnaught. Without the Light... I don't know what kind of chance your leaders stand against them."

Evelyns eyes slowly went dim as she hung her head, letting out a sigh. Netra was about to put a hand on Eves shoulder, but she hesitated and decided against it.

Eve; "... Ok... I guess... I guess I'm staying with you guys."

Eve looked to Krosis, her voice small as the latter rolled a technological sphere up the ramp to their position, putting it near the console with a purple light facing the ceiling.

Eve; "If you're ok with it, that is."

Krosis looked at Eve with a mix of pity and frustration in her eyes, looking upwards in disgruntled hum. Netra stood before speaking to Krosis.

Netra; "Mother... She needs us. And we can use her help, too."

Krosis turned her head to look at the pair, planting her lower hands on her hips.

Krosis; "Well... Better find a way to prove you're useful soon. Hard to see you doing much with only a pair of arms. Already a pair of arms short of the both of us."

Eve looked around the "room" with a hum, eyeing a couple hunks of steel shaped into I-beams.

Eve; "Hmm... If I could cut up one of those struts, I could probably make myself a couple peg legs."

Krosis looked to the I-beams and then back to the pair, Netra drawing one of her shock daggers.

Netra; "I got it!"

Netra turned on her dagger, and it buzzed with electricity arcing across the blade. She proceeded to cut two leg-length pieces from the steel, Krosis wandering over to carry the chunks to Eve.

Eve; "Thank you."

Krosis only grunted in acknowledgement as Netra returned and handed the blade to Eve. Evelyn proceeded to cut down the metal into poles, keeping the I shape towards the end to spread out her weight. She then did her best to weld the stumps to the steel, wincing a little when she got close to where the tubes in her legs were cauterized; not because she hit them, but because she was close to them.

Netra; "... Do you want me to do that, Evelyn?"

Eve glanced to Netra as she began to work on the other leg.

Eve; "I... Think I have it, thank you."

Krosis and Netra both watched as Eve whittled down the next I-beam. After half an hour of work, both legs were shaped, and Eve handed the dagger back to Netra.

Eve; "Alright... Let's see how they work."

Once she got the knife back, Netra helped Eve to her feet, letting her stand without support once she thought the Exo was stable. The Vandal took a couple steps back as Eve held out her arms to balance herself.

Netra; "... I think it worked!"

Eve laughed a little, attempting to take a step forward... And almost immediately falling flat on her face. Netra let out a quiet gasp, hand over her rebreather as Eve rolled onto herself onto her back, looking up at the two.

Eve; "Heh... I guess getting the legs on was the easy part."

Krosis shook her head out of disappointment... But her eyes betrayed a sense of approval.

Krosis; "It's a start, I suppose."

The captain let out a lone chuckle as Netra went to help Eve up again.

Chapter 9

Ca'uor stomps through the halls of his capital ship, fists clenched at his sides as he makes his way to the bridge. The door opens to Cabal scrambling back and forth, the heads of Psions on the bridge flaring with ultraviolet plasma, indicating intense thought. Ca'uor glanced to Cyrax as he turned to look at him.

Cyrax; "Val Ca'uor, Commander Kravaum and Commander Thuun are hailing from Earth."

Ca'uor rolled his eyes under his helmet as he approached the viewscreen.

Ca'uor; "Finally... On screen!"

The massive window darkened before illuminating to reveal two Cabal centurions; one wore the usual red and gold armor, but the other wore white and gold. Ca'uors helmet folded and collapsed onto his head as he scowled at them both.

Ca'uor; "I've been getting alert pings all over the system, you two! Why has Ghaul said nothing?! You first, Kravaum!"

The Cabal in red and gold cleared his throat before speaking, a touch of nervousness in his tone.

Kravaum; "I cannot speak for Ghaul, my Val; I've been stationed on Mars by order of the Dominus, in the Human city of Freehold. Though, I've been told that there's a guerrilla faction of Humans that resist us beyond the city... I've even gotten reports of one such Human around the north pole of Mars here."

Ca'uor growled under his breath, turning his gaze to the one in white and gold.

Ca'uor; "And you, Thuun?"

Thuun glanced behind himself when gunfire was heard, and alarms began to blare.

Thuun; "Val, I've just been informed there's a Human contingent attacking the city! They're en route to the Immortal as we speak!"

Ca'uor clenched his fists so tightly the leather in his palms began to tear and rip.

Ca'uor; "Well, don't just stand there, do something about it! Get me the Consul!"

Thuun pounded a fist to his chest as his camera turned off.

Cyrax; "Val... Comms to the Immortal have been left open. Encryption has not been updated for the last 2 standard hours."

Ca'uor furrowed his brow, his helmet folding and collapsing onto his shoulders.

Ca'uor; "On screen."

The half of the screen that used to show Thuun now showed the throne room on the Immortal, where Ghaul was once seen commanding the attack on the Tower... Now empty, a Human in white robes laying dead on the floor, as well as the Consul laying dead on his stomach; what could be seen of his face was pale... At least, pale for a Cabal. Ca'uors eyes widened upon seeing the Consul dead, taking a step back.

Ca'uor; "... Any Psion on that ship that can report what happened?"

Cyrax tapped some buttons on his console, reaching over to another monitor belonging to a Cabal, prompting them to give Cyrax a side-eye glare.

Cyrax; "Qatatch reports that the Consul was murdered... by the Dominus, whom is currently engaging a Guardian on the Immortals weather deck."

Ca'uor grit his teeth, growling under his breath.

Ca'uor; "Can anyone get me a view of the Dominus?!"

There was then a buzzing from Cyraxs console, and Cyrax turned back to Ca'uor.

Cyrax; "Val, we're being hailed by Commander Thuun."

Kravaum, who had remained on call this whole time, was on the edge of his seat, and shouted back to his crew at the same time as Ca'uor.

Kravaum & Ca'uor; "ON SCREEN!"

The two shared a glance before Thuuns screen flickered back on, from the perspective of a helmet camera. It zoomed in from a rooftop to the Immortals deck, watching a Guardian combat Ghaul, both wielding the Light; the Guardian tossed a Void magnetic grenade at Ghaul, their class and gender indistinguishable from the distance, while Ghaul, wearing a gray column of technology on his back, projected a shield of Void Light ahead of him, blocking the explosion of the grenade and bashing the Human away.

Ca'uor; "Why do you just stand there, Thuun! Shoot them or something!"

Thuun spoke over the audio of the stream, his breathing a little shaky.

Thuun; "The Dominus commanded that any Human to board the ship would fight him in a Rite of Proving; we cannot interfere, this fight is between them alone."

Ca'uors right eye twitched and he let out a scream before stomping the ground, shaking the bridge.

Ca'uor; "Honor be damned! I'm your superior and I'm ordering you to fire on them!"

Thuun audibly hesitated, stuttering before finally replying.

Thuun; "Yes, Val."

A Cabal rifle came into view in the lower right corner of the screen, Thuun pressing a button on the rifle to activate a rail-mounted launcher in the underbarrel of his weapon. He raised it high, a digital display giving him an arc to fire it so he could hit the Guardian square on. Just before he could fire, the Guardian produced a rocket launcher from their back and fired it at Ghaul, striking the backpack on Ghaul and making it combust, sending shrapnel all over the deck. Ghaul cried out in defiance as he fell from the sky, floundering onto the deck with a tremendous clang. Thuuns digital display turned off, leaving only the zoomed in view of the fight, lowering his weapon slowly.

Thuun; "By Acrius... No..."

Ca'uors fists finally released out of shock, his eyes wide at the sight. His breathing got heavier as he took a step back again.

Ca'uor; "It can't-"

Ca'uor was interrupted as a beam of pale yellow Light shot up from the body of Ghaul, sprouting wings before collapsing them back into a viscous, smoking apparition of Ghaul, dripping with some kind of glowing plasma.

Ca'uor; "... What the hells?"

The voice of Ghaul echoed in through Thuuns screen, the apparition facing the Traveler.

Ghaul; "TRAVELER! DO YOU SEE ME NOW?"

He then turned back to face the city, raising a hand and making a fist.

Ghaul; "I AM IMMORTAL! A GOD!"

Ghaul then looked down to his ship, where the Guardian was.

Ghaul; "YOU HAVE FAILED!"

Ghaul then raised his hands up, Ca'uor pointing at the Traveler behind Ghaul, which began to glow a light Cyan from a small crack.

Ca'uor; "What the hell is that?!"

Cyrax began typing away at the console as Ghaul shouted.

Ghaul; "WITNESS THE DAWNING OF A NEW AGE!"

Cyrax then looked back to Ca'uor, his eye wide.

Cyrax; "Cage integrity is dropping rapidly, 86% and falling!"

Ghaul turned around when more cracks appeared on the cage, shining a light on him that he had to shield his eyes from.

Ghaul; "You do... See me..."

Ghaul again screamed defiantly as the Light began to poke myriad holes in his oversized form.

Ghaul; "NOOOO!"

Thuuns screen then went white before turning off. Ca'uor gasped quietly and took a couple steps forward, tapping the screen.

Ca'uor; "... Thuun? Thuun!"

He looked back to Cyrax, who was busy tapping keys on the display.

Cyrax; "The release of Light shorted out Thuuns transmitters; he can still hear you, but you will not hear him."

Ca'uor grumbled and turned back to the monitor.

Ca'uor; "Argh... Thuun, take your forces and regroup at Mercury! Kravaum, continue your operations on Mars. We're on our own."

Kravaum nodded as his screen glitched, glowing cyan as he looked around, letting out a sigh before turning off his call.

CHAPTER 10

Among the drills deployed on Nessus by the Red Legion, a Fallen skiff flies into view, weaving and slipping through the field of drill towers, the sun beginning to rise in the distance. Inside the skiff, Eve lay on her stomach (as the space between the ceiling and floor was only a meter, give or take) with a long cable wrapped around her waist, holding onto the interior with bated breath as she watched Krosis deftly manipulate the controls.

Eve; "... Do you think they'll notice it's gone?"

Netra was heard on the other side of Krosis, crawling over to Eve and handing her a Shock pistol.

Netra; "I think it'll be pretty obvious when they see one of their two Skiffs missing."

Eve grimaced as she opened the breech of the pistol, checking the power level of the battery inside before closing it back up, accidentally bumping her head against the ceiling when Krosis made a sharp turn.

Eve; "Ow!"

Krosis glanced back to Eve and rolled all four of her eyes.

Krosis; "Careful!"

Eve glared at Krosis, massaging the back of her head.

Eve; "Thanks."

Netra crawled over to Krosis, watching the viewscreen with her, a small sphere tied to her back that appeared to be a Servitor core.

Netra; "How much longer to the primary drill?"

Krosis tapped a portion of the screen with her lower right hand, displaying a map of the drilling fields, with one of the furthest highlighted in dark blue.

Krosis; "Less than 5 minutes, so get ready to deploy."

Netra nodded and gestured for Eve to follow, the both of them crawling towards the aft of the skiff. There were 8 hatches in two columns of four along the floor at the rear of the dropship, each overlooked by a collapsible strut against the ceiling. Netra looked at Eve, whose breathing was labored out of anxiety, and she rested a hand on Eves shoulder, looking at her with a soft smile.

Netra; "It will be ok. We go in, download data, go back out, simple."

Eve let out a sigh, slipping the shock pistol onto a magnetic plate on her lower back.

Eve; "I wish I had your faith. My missions don't usually go that smoothly."

Netra let out a quiet chuckle, patting Eve on the shoulder.

Netra; "It'll be fine, I promise! My mother always gets me through, she'll make this run a success too."

Eve nodded gently, looking at Netra with a small smile.

Eve; "Thanks, hun. Really."

Before Netra could say anything further, Krosis shouted to the back of the ship, grabbing her Arc spear and pulled herself over to the rear with the pair.

Krosis; "Refraction field going off in 5, ready or not!"

Eve clenched her grip against the interior of the ship, breathing still vapid and brisk as she stared unblinking at the hatch. A kind of deep whirring was heard as the refractor powered down, and the hatch opened, followed by the struts unfolding and poking out of the hole. Netra and Krosis crawled onto the strut and slid out near simultaneously, while Eve awkwardly maneuvered herself onto it and slid down, floundering onto her back when her makeshift peg legs failed to provide traction on the hook.

She landed face first on an outcropping to one of the drills, likely a landing pad, and got to her "feet" with a grunt, holding her arms out to keep herself steady as she regained her bearings. Krosis was already walking closer to a door when Netra gestured for Eve to follow.

Netra; "C'mon, let's make it quick!"

Evelyn nodded and started slow before finding a rhythm and walking swiftly towards the door. Krosis reached into a pocket in her armor and pulled out a disk shaped piece of technology with several glowing buttons, pressing the center button and causing one half of the disk to rotate and reveal a myriad of what looked like keys. She pressed another button and then it collapsed back into its prior shape, and the door into the drill elevator opened. Eve watched with a raised eyebrow, a mix of surprise and amusement on her faceplate.

Eve; "W-what was that?"

Krosis shrugged and stepped onto the elevator, Netra remaining at Eves side until the Exo followed her in.

Krosis; "I think... Skeleton Key, is what that'd translate as. Haven't found a door it isn't able to open yet."

Netra drew a Wire rifle from under her cloak with her lower hands and thumbed the safety, leaning over so she could look at Eve, the elevator closing up and descending when Krosis tapped a button.

Netra; "It's not as good as a Sacred Splicers gauntlet, but it's still neat!"

Eve nodded with a gentle smile as the elevator door opened following a deep buzz, revealing an almost completely open control center, with a computer sitting in the middle, projecting a hologram of a Vex minotaur along with its weapon. Krosis narrowed her eyes as the trio approached the console.

Krosis; "Are they... Trying to dig up a Vex?"

Netra peered into the scope of her weapon and looked around the whole control room, keeping her finger off the trigger.

Netra; "That doesn't seem smart... No cloakers detected... For now, anyways."

Evelyn approached the computer and unwound the cable about her abdomen, plugging one end into a port in the Cabal console, running the other end into the Servitor core strapped to Netra. Netra would then hold up her upper left arm, using her lower arms to tap through screen after screen projected onto her forearm.

Netra; "Translation software is working! I'm taking everything that isn't nailed down!"

Krosis nodded with a stern expression, holding her spear with both hands as she looked around.

Krosis; "Make it quick... Don't wanna be here any longer than we have to."

Eve stood close to Netra as the data was being downloaded, ocassionally reading messages that were logged, the encryption swiftly broken by the Servitor.

Netra; "Huh... Evelyn, are you seeing this? There's mention of... An attack on the Immortal? What is that?"

Evelyn leaned in close to read the holographic screen, eyes going wide as she read the contents aloud.

Eve; "Dominus dead... Consul dead... Speaker dead? Traveler, they killed the Speaker..."

Krosis glanced to the screen, keeping watch on the horizon and the elevator.

Krosis; "Dominus? Machine above, they decapitated the empire."

Eves breathing picked up a little, her voice a mix of elated and worried.

Eve; "If there was an attack on Cabal in the City, that means the Vanguard is still alive! I can still go home!"

Before Netra can say anything, an alarm begins to blare overhead, followed by the sounds of Harvesters descending from orbit.

Netra; "Uh... I think they know we're here."

Both the Servitor screen and the Cabal console began to flash orange, and Cabal drop pods began to crash into the open command center, dissolving to reveal three trios of Legionaries, each armed with what appeared to be shotguns of some kind.

Eve; "Get down!"

Both Eve and Netra were able to hit the deck before the shots reached them. Krosis, meanwhile, remained standing and unharmed, her face twisting into an angered snarl, and nabbed the shock pistol off Eves back with her lower right hand to fire a few shots at the Cabal. The bolts did minimal damage to the Cabal armor, but one shot to the helmet of one of the Legionaries caused it to depressurize and shatter off their head, exposing their face in a rush of oil and fumes, promptly falling over. More shots from the Cabal rang out, and Krosis finally took cover when a few of the projectiles from the shotguns knocked the armor off her shoulder.

Netra attempted to briefly take aim and fire her Wire Rifle in her upper arms, firing at the Legionaries and stunning them when the shots hit their armor, leaving deep plasma burns and melted craters in the carapace. Krosis collapsed her Arc spear onto her back as she poked her head back up over the console, taking another few potshots at the Legionaries.

Krosis; "Netra, bring the ship around! That'll make them think twice!"

Netra shoved her Wire rifle into Eves hands as she brought up the display on her arm again.

Netra; "Yes, mother!"

Eve fumbled the weapon a moment before leveling it behind cover and taking a few shots, doming one of the Legionaries and taking them out, but still leaving 7 Cabal to slowly advance on their position, still laying down heavy fire. Soon, Netra directed the Skiff to remotely fly around from the landing pad to the opposite end, coming into view and deploying four bouncing spheres that trailed Arc plasma before detonating near the Cabal. The explosions took out the central trio of Cabal, but the Skiff was soon knocked from the sky by a Harvester, sending the craft tumbling towards the ground and getting torn up by the drills below. Netra let out a defeated whimper when she saw the Harvester replace the

Skiff in the air, the side hatches opening up and deploying four Phalanxes, their shields activating once they stepped onto the drill.

Netra; "Wh-... What now? They're gonna kill us!"

Krosis let out a frustrated sigh as she hid further behind cover, the Phalanxes laying down fire from behind their shields with carbines that shot miniature rockets.

Krosis; "Uh... If I had one of those shields, I could actually do something, this pistol isn't doing crap!"

Eves eyes then went wide as she remained behind cover, as if everything else became muted around her. She looked around, trying to discern the direction of the feeling of pressure on her person; it seemed to come from everywhere within and without. She mumbled, unheard from the gunfire.

Eve; "... Do you guys feel that? It's... Like I'm coming up for air..."

Suddenly, a wave of cyan plasma washed across the landscape, making the Cabal cease firing as they attempted to determine amongst themselves what occurred. Netra looked to her mother and Eve, eyes wide.

Netra; "... What was that? Eve, are you ok?"

Eve let out a breathless chuckle, holding up her hands as they began to hum with Void Light.

Eve; "... I'm better than ok."

She turned back to the Cabal, still disoriented, and disappeared in a flurry of Void Light, the coil of cable dropping to the ground. Netra raised an eyebrow and waved her upper left hand through where Eve once was. Krosis glanced between where Eve disappeared and the Cabal stood, only to see Eve reappear in an eruption of Void plasma, disintegrating all the Phalanxes in one go. The four Legionaries that weren't caught in the initial explosion spoke in their native tongue before opening fire on Eve. She Blinked out of the way of the first round of shotgun blasts, sending a sphere of Void Light to the right that combusted with such force both the Legionaries were thrown from the platform, down to the drills below.

Krosis and Netra watched with horror and awe, respectively, as Eve then tossed a Vortex grenade towards the last pair of Cabal. They both ducked and it went past them, one of them letting out a haughty chuckle, before the grenade detonated on the ground and pulled them both into its radius, disintegrating them into quantum particles in mere seconds. Evelyn then turned to look at Netra and Krosis, her smile going down when she saw the expression on Krosiss face. The commotion prompted the Harvester to reposition, and Eve turned to face it with clenched fists. She raised her arms overhead, materializing a Nova Bomb and hurling it at the Harvester, blasting out the integrated cockpit and causing the vessel to list and eventually crash into the control room, making a haphazard bridge off the drill to the surface of Nessus.

Eve; "Go, go!"

Eve wildly gestured for the pair to follow, and they leapt up from behind cover to follow Evelyn off the drill, Netra wresting the cable out of the console as she ran. The trio made their way towards the forests of Nessus in the distance, stopping only briefly to see an immense, golden craft shaped like a triangular maw enter orbit of the planetoid. Once deep in the woods, they stopped under one of the larger trees, all of them collapsing to the ground from exhaustion; Krosis taking a knee, Eve floundering to the ground on her back and Netra dropping to all... sixes. She pauses a moment to catch her breath before speaking, eyes looking up to the large ship in orbit.

Netra; "... I don't even wanna know whose ship that is."

Krosis took a few deep deep breaths, extending her spear and pulling herself to her feet whilst using it for support.

Krosis; "... I don't know... But, you-"

She then pointed to Eve.

Krosis; "You didn't kill us, you absolutely could have... Why?"

Eve remained laying on her back, breathing heavily also as she turned her head to look at Krosis, doing her best to express sincerity.

Eve; "... I don't want to. Just because... Eliksni have taken from me... That doesn't mean I hate all Eliksni."

She turned her eyes to Netra, whom looked at Eve simultaneously.

Eve; "... Some, I like a lot."

The sentence made Netras cheeks subtly glow a dim blue with Ether, mimicking the blush of a Human as she looked away bashfully.

CHAPTER 11

The room was disgustingly lavish in decor, bedight in gold and white sandstone and the floor littered with blobs of a purple, genatinous substance strewn about. In the middle of it all sat a Cabal in golden armored robes, jeweled chalice in his right hand and an amethyst stamped to his forehead with a gold plate. He downed the last of the fluid in the chalice, also containing the lavender colored gelatin, smacking his lips together as best a Cabal could. He furrowed his brow in a bored expression before standing from the throne, letting the chalice hang down at his side as he walked out of the throne room, out of an immense gold and marble door, leading out to an impressive courtyard that was overlooked by a massive statue of the same Cabal.

He approached the statue and dragged a fingeracross the largest toenail, looking at his finger and frowning at the layer of dust on it. He looked upwards to see a shield of plasma between the courtyard and the passing blueshifted stars overhead. He took in a deep breath and turned to one of the other doors in the courtyard, making his way over to it as a deep warble was heard overhead; a stray asteroid burning up against the plasma shield at relativistic speeds. He didn't visibly acknowledge it as the door opened and he descended a staircase lit by torch scones that burned with sulfur blue flame.

At the bottom of the steps, he entered into a theatre of sorts, a grid of white plasma set up in front of the stage that seemed to contain a large Vex minotaur, its chassis weathered like oxidized copper. He sat in a throne at the back of the theatre, letting out a slow exhale as he watched the Minotaur wander back and forth. The Cabal spoke, seemingly to the Minotaur, but it didn't acknowledge him at first.

Cabal; "Oh, my beloved Hasapiko... We're nearly in the Sol system. I hope that my Shadows have been productive apart from me."

He let out a chuckle, eyes cast towards the front row of the theatre.

Cabal; "Perhaps we will find more of your kind here, away from the star forge."

Hasapiko paused and looked at the Cabal, letting out a quick sequence of squawks and warbles, prompting another chuckle from the Cabal.

Cabal; "Maybe I'll let you go free, find your own tribe of Vex to comingle with... Oh, but how I would miss your little constructs and talkative episodes."

Hasapiko beeped and groaned as they stood with a straight posture, their head perking up and scanning to the right, a red cone of light shining forward at the wall. The Cabal let out a huff of amusement before raising an eyebrow upon hearing footsteps to the left, looking to see a Psion in purple and gold armor running over, kotowing once they reached the throne. They remained on the floor for a full 15 seconds before standing, looking up at the Cabal with a combination of reverence and exhaustion. The Cabal could hear her voice in her mind, also sounding exhausted from her apparent sprint through the halls.

Psion; "Oh mighty and glorious Calus, Emperor of all joys, Prince of mirth, Champion of cheer, Lord of laughter, Master of celebrations, the good host with-"

Calus held up a hand to stop the Psion from speaking, smiling as he looked at her.

Calus; "You may dispense with the formalities, Turok. What news do you bring?"

Turok took a couple heavy breaths before regaining her posture, clasping her hands behind her back.

Turok; "We've heard back from Kravaum, your double-agent... Ghaul is dead, but not from the Shadows."

His smile turned to confusion, and Calus stood from the throne.

Calus; "Walk with me to the bridge... Who finished him off, then?"

Turok would follow Calus to the bridge as they both re-cieved a vision of the computer viewing from Kravaum; Ghaul being shot from the sky by a rocket fired by a Guardian on the ground, slamming into the hull of the Immortal with a tremendous clang. Calus laughed as the vision faded, and they were now on their way to the bridge through another door that was in the courtyard.

Calus; "Such a small thing to fell such a mighty gladiator! You would hardly think it a threat, and yet... What is it?"

Turok slowed her pace so Calus could walk ahead of her.

Turok; "A Human, native to the system. We don't know their subspecies or tribe, all we know is their wield incredible magic, nothing like we've seen before."

Calus let out a hum of contemplation as they made their way onto the bridge that was still opulent in appearance, busy with more Psions and guarded by a pair of Centurions, also donned in gold and purple armor. The blueshifting of the viewport gave way to a view of Nessus, pale green atmos-phere contrasted by autumn colored trees and blocky patches of Vex concrete exposed to space. Turok approached one of the bridge screens and tapped a few buttons, looking back to Calus with a surprised expression.

Turok; "Your eminence, there's a fleet of ships gathering on the other side of the planetoid. Ten, to be precise."

Calus took a couple steps closer, letting out a laugh.

Calus; "Ten ships? Red Legion, I presume?"

Turok nodded, pulling up a projection of the fleet.

Turok; "Yes. The highest-ranking member registers as Val... Ca'uor."

Calus again laughed, resting his hands on his stomach.

Calus; "They've only a Val to lead them? They will not get far... But, I would hate to lose so many of my loyal subjects in a war of attrition, not to mention I only have so many automatons."

Turok tilted her head out of curiosity, flipping through a few windows on the monitor before turning back to Calus.

Turok; "Your eminence, Red Legion comms report a rogue Human on Nessus, accompanied by a couple of Eliksni. They seem to also wield the magic that killed Ghaul. If just one could kill Ghaul..."

Calus grew a smirk on his face.

Calus; "One would certainly be more than enough for a Val."

He put a hand on his chin in thought, turning around to look at the bridge crew before his eyes landed on the Centurion to his left.

Calus; "You; remove your helmet and tell me your name."

The Centurion lifted his helmet up the way one may raise the hood of a car, pulling a rebreather from his mouth.

Centurion; "Uh, Thot'gor, your eminence."

Calus nodded with a smile.

Calus; "Take one of the pleasure barges and travel to the planetoid... Locate this Human and promise them riches in exchange for taking care of Ca'our; whatever their little heart desires."

Thot'gor put his helmet back on, setting the rebreather back in his mouth and saluting by banging a fist to his chest.

Thot'gor; "Of course, your eminence; they'll be here as soon as possible."

As Thot'gor left the bridge, Turok turned to Calus, folding her arms over her chest.

Turok; "Um... Where are you going, my Emperor?"

Calus laughed, turning to leave the bridge, holding up the chalice he'd been brandishing this whole time as though it were afixed to his arm.

Calus; "To get a refill... And prepare a feast for my future guests."

CHAPTER 12

Evelyn, Krosis and Netra stalk their way across the Nessu-sian landscape at night, weapons in hand. Krosis leaned over to Eve and whispered as she turned on the head of her spear, Arc bolts jumping across the blade.

Krosis; "... Evelyn?"

Eve looked back to Krosis, smiling sheepishly.

Eve; "Yes, captain?"

Krosis used her lower right hand to gingerly hold Eves chin, turning her head to look her in the eyes, Evelyn swallowing hard.

Krosis; "We've been tracking this Cabal for almost 5 months, and three months before that were spent on the run ever since you got your Light back. We *need* a re-supply more than any communication doohickey, understand? Even if we don't get a comms unit off this guy, you're helping us take their loot, understand?"

Evelyn nodded, blinking rapidly as Krosis stared her down.

Eve; "Yes, ma'am."

Krosis gestured to the entrance to a cave with her lower left hand, bordered by Vex metal and concrete.

Krosis; "You take lead, you garner more attention than either of us. We'll have your back."

Evelyn nodded again, giving no verbal reply as she proceeded into the cave, white knuckle grip on a shrapnel launcher. Netra came to stand alongside her mother, taking in a deep breath before speaking.

Netra; "... Why do you still speak to her like she's a Dreg?"

Krosis let out an unamused huff, restraining a smirk.

Krosis; "She still thinks like a Human; One task that must be completed, nothing else matters. If she's going to survive with us, she must think like an Eliksni; considerations as many as our fingertips. The better she can see the whole picture, the better she'll survive with us."

Netra nodded in understanding, readying her Wire rifle and following Evelyn into the cave, Krosis taking the rear. Evelyn walked past a large Vex sphere to the left in a large puddle of radiolaria before clambering up a wall of Vex metal and tech to see a large space made of alien bronze and concrete. She looked around with narrow eyes, steadying her breathing as she took cover behind a pillar of Vex copper, peering around it to see a Legionary and a Psion standing guard over a flight of stairs leading to a pathway with geysers of radiolarian fluid, being patrolled by further Legionaries, Incendiors, Psions and a Colossus at the far back, flanked by a pair of war beasts. Krosis and Netra remained hidden near the entrance to the larger room, Eve looking their way.

Evelyn made a gesture to the pair to stay in place, while she thumbed the safety on her shrapnel launcher before jumping into the open. Krosis silently reached out a free hand as if to stop Eve, but let her arm hang down with a quiet snarl. Almost as soon as Evelyn stepped out of cover, the Psion and Legionary at the top of the stairs turned to look at Evelyn, speaking in an alien tongue both. Before they could level weapons, Eve let loose several volleys of searing hot alloy scraps from her weapon into the Psion, felling them after the first few bursts and screaming all the while. She prepared to fire at the Legionary now... But only heard a click, indicating an empty magazine.

The Legionary let out a chortle, drawing their slug rifle and preparing to fire, only being stopped by Netra landing a headshot on them. Eve let out a sigh of relief before leaping to the bottom of the stairs to see the gunfire had attracted the attention of the rest of the Cabal. Krosis shouted at her as the Incendiors readied their weapons.

Krosis; "Fall back, Evelyn! Stay near us!"

Evelyn looked back as she stood at the bottom of the stairs, making a gesture with her left hand and creating a circle of Light at her feet that flowed delicately out from a central point at her feet.

Eve; "It's alright, captain; I can handle-"

She cut herself off as a Void sphere from one of the Psions deployed itself at her feet, sending her into the air as it erupted, shortly after getting knocked back by a concussive shockwave from the nearest Incendior. Eve landed near Netra and Krosis, throwing off her robes that were now set alight, breathing erratically. Netra came over to Evelyns aid as Krosis rolled her eyes, using her lower right arm to toss a mine pulled from her back, chucking it the same way one may hurl a discus. The mine launches a ball that sparks and crackles with electricity into the air, hovering a moment before exploding with a blinding flash, disorienting the Cabal that were ready to attack.

Netra; "Are you hurt?!"

With her burning articles of clothing removed, Evelyn had only a purple tube bra on to cover her bosom, which she covered with her arms as Netra pulled her into cover.

Eve; "I think I'm ok... I think."

While the Cabal were blinded, Krosis leapt out of cover with her spear and jabbed it into the fuel tank of one of the Incendiors, ripping it off their back and throwing it at the other, causing a fiery explosion and killing them, along with a pair of Psions that were near them. When the original Incendior attempted to melee Krosis with the barrel of their weapon, she was able to dodge out of the way and jam the spear into their neck, causing a spray of black fluid to come out. She then ran back to the stairs and retrieved a slug rifle from the first fallen Psion, using it as a sidearm to fire back at the various Cabal, reinforcements emerging from adjacent, smaller rooms and doorways at the sides and rear of the main area. When Netra pulled Eve to her "feet", Krosis grabbed Eve by the chin, more forcefully than before.

Krosis; "Stop thinking like a Dreg! Don't keep all your focus on one thing; think strategically, not tactically! That's how you survive!"

She let go of Evelyn with a growl, and Eve nodded slowly.

Eve; "I understand... I'm sorry."

Krosis tossed the slug rifle to Eve, letting out a frustrated sigh.

Krosis; "Don't apologize yet; not until we're out of this mess!"

She peered around the corner, seeing the further reinforcements that have entered the room, looking back to Eve and Netra with a stern expression, putting the spear in her upper hands as her lower left adjusted her Ether mask.

Krosis; "Alright... Evelyn, use your Light and make a show, distract the Cabal. Netrasiik, cover her; I'm going for the Partisan."

Eve gave a salute, while Netra gave a stiff nod, but they both spoke in unison.

Eve & Netra; "Yes, captain!"

They shared a glance with a small smile before Eve Blinked away in a surge of electricity and Arc Light, morphing into a sphere of electrons and lightning. She sped down the stairs once more, getting close to reinforcing Phalanxes before transforming back into her Exo form, sending lightning strikes surging upwards from the ground all around her, some of the strikes disintegrating the Phalanxes and leaving their shields to clatter to the ground. This drew the attention of the newly arrived Legionaries, and Eve stomped the ground as her body became charged with Arc Light, bearing a snarl on her faceplate (or the Exo equivalent). As Evelyn Blinked and sprinted around, electrocuting Cabal and drawing attention to herself, Netra remained in cover, sniping any Cabal that attempted to flank or otherwise attack beyond her periphery.

Krosis, meanwhile, slinked towards the rear of the room, spear firmly grasped in her upper hands. The Colossus was distracted by watching Evelyn use the Light to decimate the reinforcements, their eye catching Netrasiik playing sharp-shooter towards the other end of the room. He took hold of a rip cord on the left side of his armor with his left hand and pulled on it, much the same way one may make a fist pump gesture, his jet pack releasing four missiles that flew up and then towards Netras position. Krosis was ready to get the attention of the Colossus before the missiles were fired... But, after seeing he was attacking her daughter first, she instead slashed at the back of the knee joints, making the Partisan shout and crumple to the ground with cries of pain, dropping their weapon.

Krosis then rolled the Colossus onto their back and kicked off their helmet as she stood on his abdomen, jamming the spear into their mouth and giving the blade a twist, the body of the Cabal briefly seizing up before going limp. She let out a sigh as she then looked back to the pair, seeing Netra snipe a Psion out of the air as Eve shoved her arms through a Phalanx shield to electrocute them. Eve looked around with the slug rifle leveled, taking a deep breath before tossing it to the ground, looking to Netra.

Eve; "Clear... Area secured."

Netra emerged from cover, slotting the wire rifle onto her back as she approached Evelyn, looking at Krosis standing on the body of the Colossus, pouting a little with her upper hands crossed over her chest.

Netra; "I thought we were supposed to interrogate him."

Krosis let out a scoff, pulling her spear from Cabals mouth, fragments of spinal column and teeth following.

Krosis; "He attacked you, I wasn't about to take that lying down."

Eve looked to Krosis with a smile, hugging her tightly, and Netra hesitantly returned the gesture.

Eve; "You're alive, that's what matters."

Netras cheeks became slightly flushed, Ether blue, intensifying when Eve planted a soft kiss on Netras cheek. The

Eliksni paused a moment, a hand gingerly coming up to where she was kissed before attempting to mimic the gesture, resulting in the clack of polymer rebreather against metal, elliciting a laugh from Eve, but she leaned into the affectionate gesture regardless.

CHAPTER 13

In orbit of Nessus, a Legionary stood guard on a landing zone on the Leviathan, weapon pointed upward. The only sound he heard was his breathing inside his helmet, turning his head to look at the thin green line that was the Nessusian horizon. He narrowed his eyes at the sight of what appeared to be a new star in the sky... Then another. And another; Ten in total. His eyes widened when he realized they were Red Legion warships, and he brought up his other arm to tap a button on his helmet.

Legionary; "Emperor, the usurpers are here! I repeat, the usurp-"

He's cut off by a drop pod slamming onto him, crushing another Legionary on the other side of the walkway as well. There were several other Legionaries further back that turned to see the sudden appearance of Val Ca'uor out of the drop pod, the cruisers behind him opening fire on the Leviathan.

Ca'uor could be heard laughing in the helmets of the Loyalists as he broadcast his comms.

Ca'uor; "Make way for the new Emperor of the Cabal! Surrender or say hi to the Vex down there!"

The Legionaries said nothing as they readied their weapons and opened fire with Slug Rifles, harmlessly bouncing off Ca'uors shield gleaming white around him. He stomped through their ranks with boisterous laughter, firing at them with his Magma launcher and occasionally grabbing them and throwing them off the deck towards Nessus. Towards the entry to the Leviathan proper, a pair of Colossi stood with railguns in hand, underslung. One of them pulled a ripcord on their shoulder to release missiles, and the rockets flew towards Ca'uor, exploding against the shield. Ca'uor let out a chuckle and retaliated by firing a blast of heated gasses at the offending Colossus, knocking them backwards and using his jetpack to lunge at the second Colossus, stomping on their abdomen with... Silence, because they're in vacuum. He screamed into his comms as the warships came closer to the bridge spire of the Leviathan.

Ca'uor; "Tear this ship a new asshole! I want it in ribbons by the time Calus is dead!"

More drop pods rained down onto the walkway, releasing Cabal Gladiators with blades in hand, running to the maintenance door, Ca'uor using his magma launcher to melt it open. The gladiators rushed in, using their blades to cut pipes that concealed bundles of wires and flows of fluids, raucous laughter filling the halls. The Leviathan rumbled and groaned as it's innards were lacerated and severed, its immense maw beginning to glow a firey orange and red as it powered on. The centaurs crust began to buckle and crack before parts and chunks began to drift upwards into the maw of the golden vessel. So many were dragged up into the furnace of the Leviathan that the core was open to space.-On the surface, Krosis, Eve and Netra ran atop one of the massive Vex concrete blocks as a pack of Warbeasts ran after them, their handlers chasing behind them atop a Goliath tank. The trio of Eve, Netra and Krosis reached the end of the block, and Eve ignited herself in Solar Light, holding out both hands and spraying the flames at the other end of another block, the Light manifesting as freshly forged metal, making a sheet of Solar alloy to bridge the gap. The three of them cross the bridge with haste, Eve lobbing a Solar grenade at the middle of the bridge and melting away the middle, causing the bridge to collapse. Netra stands there with her upper hands on her knees, breathing heavily and fanning off her face with her upper right hand.

Netra; "They can't make it across... Can they?"

On the other side, a Centurion in gold and red armor approached the edge, kicking one of the Warbeasts aside.

Centurion; "... Why have we halted? Give chase, they're right there!"

One of the Legionaries approached, reloading their slug shotgun.

Legionary; "Sir, the bridge has been taken out, we've no way across."

One could imagine the Centurion rolling his eyes under his helmet, followed by a scoff.

Centurions; "You nimrod! We have jetpacks!"

The Legionary attempted to stop the Centurion from taking off, but it was in vain, as a jet of orange flames shot out from the pack on his back, sending him towards the trio on the other side of the gap. Netra watched with wide eyes, Krosis leveling her Arc spear and Eve watching with Solar Light still in her hands. They watch as the Centurion gets closer and closer still... Then begins to lose lift as his pack fails to keep him aloft, and he falls to the ground between the blocks screaming. The Legionary leans over the gap and watches the Centurion fall.

Legionary; "... They're jump-packs, not jet-packs."

Meanwhile, Krosis, Netra and Eve made their way down the block closer to the surface, at a slower pace now that the Cabal weren't behind them. Netrasiik took an Ether canister off her back and took in a deep inhale, taking a couple breaths afterwards before speaking up.

Netra; "So... What're we gonna do? We've no way off Nessus and it's getting pulled apart by that... Thing, up there."

Krosis let out a huff of disappointment, glancing to the Leviathan overhead.

Krosis; "I'm accepting any ideas; most crews would've fled to the far side of the centaur by now, and I doubt we have long until the whole thing is sucked up."

There was then a boom overhead, as though something were entering atmosphere. Eve looked first, the other two Eliksni looking shortly thereafter, seeing a large ship of white metal and gold plating, a pair of sails at the front also covered in gold leaf. The three had their respective weapons at the ready, except for Eve, who had Void Light in her palms, as the ship descended and settled in just under the tree line, its thrusters kicking up dust for only a moment as Vex concrete and metal was exposed underneath. A ramp lowered on the underbelly as a Cabal Centurion jumped down in black and gold armor, a purple loin cloth about their waist. He turned to look at the trio, tapping a panel on his helmet.

Centurion; "This translator working?"

Only Netra lowered her weapon, while Eve kept Void Light in her hands, but took on a less defensive posture.

Eve; "You're not Red Legion."

The Centurion raised his hands in capitulation, shaking his head.

Centurion; "Oh, perish the thought! I wouldn't touch those traitors with a 50 foot pole, thank you. But, I'm actually here to talk to you about them."

Krosis took another step forward, keeping a white-knuckle grip on her spear.

Krosis; "Speak, ba sloat."

The Centurion somewhat sneered at Krosis.

Centurion; "You kiss your mother with that mouth?"

Krosis snarled, and the Centurion let out an awkward chuckle.

Centurion; "Yeah, uh... Bracus Thot'gor, Centurion of the True Cabal Emperor. On behalf of his joyous majesty, he's offering great bounties and rewards to any Human that can kill the rogue Val, Ca'uor, and prevent his Leviathan from being shot down."

Krosis finally lowered her spear, jabbing it into the ground like a hiking implement, turning to look at Eve. Evelyn, meanwhile, puts a hand on her chin to think, looking to the pair of Eliksni.

Eve; "They're asking for a Guardian specifically... You guys can stay on the ship."

Netra shook her head, putting her weapon on her back.

Netra; "You've done so much for us... The least we can do is help you one last time."

Krosis sighed as Netra turned to look at her, nodding gently.

Krosis; "It's our one ticket off the planetoid, might as well make myself useful."

Eve smiled and then looked to Thot'gor, shaking off the Void Light in her hands.

Eve; "Tell the Emperor he's got a deal."

CHAPTER 14

A board the Leviathan bridge, Calus stood to overlook a fleet of 10 Red Legion ships, their deck guns aimed squarely at the bridge of the much larger vessel, as if aimed at Calus himself. He let out a melancholy sigh, straightening his posture as he stood upright, hearing a door open behind him. He turned to look and saw Val Ca'uor walking through the immense doors of polished sandstone and gold, magma launcher in his off hand by the handguard. Ca'uor laughed, outstretching his arms as he spoke.

Ca'uor; "This is all that the mighty emperor has brought to bear to protect himself? Shoulda invested more in that cloning tech than all that gold!"

Calus rolled his eyes, folding his arms over his chest as the door closed behind Ca'uor.

Calus; "And you would invest in further conquests? What of your people back on Torobatl? Would you have them languish while you gather glory and trophies for yourself? *My*

Torobatl was a prosperous Torobatl! The Cabal did not know hunger nor thirst, only joy; why else exile me instead of killing me?"

Ca'uor snarled as he approached, his helmet unfolding from around his head.

Ca'uor; "I can only guess that Ghaul and Caiatl exiled you because they were weak! I woulda had you fed to the Leviathans back home had I been in charge of the coup!"

Calus only laughed, leaning his head back a little as a smile came across his face, doing his best to not acknowledge the pleasure barge approaching the landing zone just outside the window, just within his periphery.

Calus; "Your ambition truly knows no bounds, does it, Val? Perhaps Ghaul was right to not promote you; I would have given you the same... Discipline as the Consul."

Ca'uor growled and stomped up to the observation platform with Calus, close enough that they could study the detail in each others faces.

Ca'uor; "You claim opulence and excess, Calus, but you scurried to this small planetoid to make your precious wine! Look around you; Vex technology on Mercury, energy on Mars... This system is rich in spoils, if one knows where to look."

He shrugged his shoulders in exasperation.

Ca'uor; "Even if you cannot control the Traveler, the people it defends would make fine labor, like the Psions."

Calus let out a quiet growl, leaning forward, keeping his arms crossed.

Calus; "The Psions were to be freed from Imperial service before I was exiled, you know. They would have had the choice to leave the empire. What do you offer, Ca'uor?"

Ca'uor only chuckled as he took his magma launcher in hand, finger on the trigger; Calus didn't budge.

Ca'uor; "The Psions, the Terrans and Eliksni, anyone that joins the Cabal will have everything! Everything you couldn't give'em! They don't like it... They, can, burn!"

He fires the magma launcher at Calus with a concussive blast of noxious fumes and burning droplets of fuel. When the smoke clears, Calus is revealed to have been an automaton, synthetic flesh melting and peeling away to expose wire frame and a metal faceplate, glowing red eyes. Ca'uors expression dropped, and Calus laughed, the automaton laughing at a slight delay as it began to spark from the burned electronics.

Calus; "You no longer amuse me, Ca'uor... My more accomodating guests have arrived to usher you out."

Behind the closed door, Thot'gor is transmatted in wearing Red Legion armor, putting the helmet over his head just as the door opens again, in time to watch Ca'uor bash the robot Calus to the ground with a backhand and a shout of anger. When Ca'uor looked back to the door to see the disguised

Thot'gor there, he shouted with a closed fist at his side, keeping his magma launcher in his right hand.

Ca'uor; "Wha'd'ya want?! I thought I told you, all personnel claim the ships fuel reserves!"

Thot'gor hesitated a little, anxiously rubbing his hands together.

Thot'gor; "Well, uh, Valus sir, there's a situation in the gardens; a communications blackout, a lot of Psions and Legionaries have gone dark and they haven't reported back. They sent me to come and get you."

Ca'uor had his helmet wrap around his head with a sigh as he descended from the observation platform, twisting a valve on his magma launcher before it sprung back into place, the fluid in the tanks on his back sloshing around a bit more.

Ca'uor; "Gotta do everything myself around here, huh?"

He pushed Thot'gor aside as he walked down the hallway and activated his bubble shield, Thot'gor waiting until he rounded the corner to hold up his right arm, whispering into his comms device.

Thot'gor; "*The beast has the scent, I repeat, the beast has the scent... Good luck.*"

Ca'uor walked the halls, through the castellum before descending a staircase into the gardens, a pale blue mist lazily hanging in the air between pillars of stone and trees with sea green leaves. But the scenery wasn't the first thing Ca'uor noticed; it was Eliksni scrapwork on the ground ahead of him, made from gold and metal plates pulled from maintenance tunnels. He approached the plate of metal with apprehension, narrowing his eyes under his helmet. He took in a deep breath before lurching forward and stepping on the plate. In milliseconds, eight spheres of metal shot up from the dirt, suspended by a stream of electricity connecting them to the ground. Ca'uor barely had time to react and register what the devices were before they exploded in a shower of sparks and electrons, creating a haze that obscured his vision and causing his shield to distort and become perforated.

Outside of the electric field, Evelyn leapt from one of the trees onto the back of Ca'uor, grabbing hold of a small piece of tech between the fuel tanks and his jump pack and ripping it off, causing the shield to finally go down. When the blurring field of quantum particles faded, Ca'uor reached behind himself to grab Eve by the arm, flinging her away and into one of the stone pillars. Evelyn slammed into the rock with a shout of pain, falling onto her stomach before slowly getting up, looking Ca'uor in the face as he laughed and pointed at her.

Ca'uor; "That's what Calus wants to kill me? Think you're some kind of space marine?"

He laughed again, taking his magma launcher in hand.

Ca'uor; "You'll be as good as smoldering iron by the time I'm done with you!"

He fired a gout of flames and fuel at her, and she narrowly dodged it by Blinking to the side with a flash of Void Light, shaking off the plasma in favor of Solar Light, extending a Dawnblade in her right hand and rushing forward to cut the fuel line connecting the weapon to the tanks on Ca'uors back. She couldn't make it before Ca'uor backhanded her away into a tree, searing an imprint of herself into the bark on impact. While Ca'uor was distracted by Eve, Krosis leapt from another treetop. spear in her upper hands as she slashed downwards against Ca'uors armor, cleaving the his belt in twain and causing his armored loincloth to drop. Ca'uor turned to look where his belt fell, then at Krosis with a growl, taking a swing with his magma launcher to bludgeon her. Quickly, she swapped the spear to her lower arms and jammed the speartip into the front grip of the weapon, then using both of her upper hands to slam her fists against his helmet with a tremendous crack, making the two of them recoil from pain.

Ca'uors helmet was cracked like an eggshell, and he used his free hand to rip it off of his face with a vicious roar, while Krosis massaged her hands, the chitin of her palms cracked as well. Just as Ca'uor prepared to fire his magma launcher at Krosis, but then Netrasiik fell from above, her cloak in her lower hands. She landed squarely on Ca'uors shoulders, covering his face with her cloak as she drew a pair of shock daggers, jabbing one into each of Ca'uors fuel tanks. The sparks caused the fuel in the tanks to ignite and send Netra flying into the air, Ca'uor being launched forwards and past Eve and Netra.

Ca'uor; "WAAAAAAAGH!"

He smashes into one of the stone pillars, knocking it over and rolling onto his back. While that was occurring, Eve flew up on Solar wings to catch Netra midair and carry her gently back to the ground. Once back on solid ground, Ca'uor sat up with a groan, standing and pulling a small handle from his back, extending a small utility knife.

Ca'uor; "Makin' a fool outta me, huh? You won't get away with that! I'll have all your skulls mounted in the bridge of my ship!"

He narrowed his eyes, subtly pointing the blade at Eve.

Ca'uor; "Do you even have a skull?"

Eve raised a hand with a finger pointing up, apprehensively preparing to speak, but Ca'uor interrupted her.

Ca'uor; "Y'know what, it doesn't matter!"

Eve lowered her hand with a sigh as Netra, Krosis and Ca'uor rush at each other near simultaneously, the Cabal able to parry and engage both the Eliksni at once with just his utility knife. When Krosis attempted a stab, Ca'uor headbutt the Eliksni and made her stagger backwards, losing her grip on the spear as she leaned back against one of the trees, a hand to her head. Netra attempted to climb up onto Ca'uor to stab his face with her shock daggers, but Ca'uor slashed at her face, slicing her outer left eye. She let out a cry of pain as she fell down to her back, letting go of her daggers and holding a pair of hands to her face. Krosis saw this and growled, galloping towards Ca'uor on all fours as Eve used a cone of Void Light to pull Ca'uors arm to keep him from delivering a killing blow on Netra. When Krosis reached Ca'uor, she picked up the spear and slashed at Ca'uors neck, spattering the nearby sandstone wall with black blood. Ca'uor immediately held a hand to his neck, dropping the knife as gurgling was heard from him.

Krosis then leapt at Ca'uor, tackling him onto his back and using all four of her arms to jam the spear into the Cabals mouth with a shout. Ca'uors eyes were wide with fear, a hand reaching for Krosis as she speared his face; a twist of the blade, and Ca'uor went limp. She stared at him with a furrowed brow, still quietly growling as she watched the blood leak from the wound in his neck. Meanwhile, Eve went over to Netra and held her in her arms, a hand on Netras face.

Eve; "Are you ok?"

Netra nodded, breathing heavily as she kept the left side of her face covered.

Netra; "Yeah... I-I think so. Just stings..."

She let out a breathless chuckle as Thot'gor entered the gardens from the door Ca'our entered through prior.

Netra; "At least I still have depth perception."

Eve chuckled quietly as Thot'gor approached the pair, glancing between them and Krosis still standing on the body of Ca'uor.

Thot'gor; "That was... Pretty fast. Uh, His Joyous Majesty would like to speak to you three, now that the... Deed is done."

Krosis retracted the spear, collapsing it and setting it on a mount on her back as Eve and Netra looked to Thot'gor.

Krosis; "Good riddance for that one."

Chapter 15

E velyn, Netra, Krosis and Thot'gor (now wearing his usual purple and gold armor) approach a massive gold and sandstone door, intricately decorated in almost obscene amounts of gold. Thot'gor leaned over to a scanner in the shape of a Cabal mouth opened wide; Caluss mouth, specifically. A fan of yellow light scanned over his retina and the monolithic doors opened to reveal Calus standing in front of mountains of gold and artifacts, outstretching his arms with a laugh.

Calus; "Welcome to my favorite vault aboard this vessel, my champions!"

The three of them entered as Thot'gor remained outside the vault, the door still open. Eve made eye contact with Calus and immediately saluted, which prompted Calus to laugh again.

Calus; "You may be at ease, Guardian! You've done me a great service, and I open this vault just for you and your allies."

Eve dropped her hand with a sheepish smile, bringing her hands together in front of her waist, looking at Netrasiik who had removed one of the cloth straps from around her upper right arm to cover her wounded eye.

Eve; "Oh, yes, Emperor, uh... Calus... Sir."

Calus chuckled and knelt down so he was close to eye level with Eve, a smile on his face.

Calus; "I like you already."

He stood back up to see Krosis rummaging through a pile of gold cubes with her spear, looking to Calus when he stood.

Krosis; "So, like... What am I allowed to take here? Any old thing?"

Calus nodded with an open mouth smile, gesturing to the larger piles of gold in the background.

Calus; "Whatever your heart desires, my four armed friend! I only ask that you take one item, be it big or small."

Calus turned to look at Netra as the Psion Turok jogged into the room with a golden box in her hands, kneeling before Calus with labored breathing. Just in time, Calus turned and picked up the box, handing it to Netra.

Calus; "This, however, is for you; for your bravery, and to symbolize your bond to the Guardian."

Netra hesitantly took the box from Turok, opening it to reveal a small sphere that looked like a prosthetic eye, glowing a dim purple. She let out a quiet gasp, looking up to Calus and giving a quick bow.

Netra; "Thank you, Emperor. I'll forever be grateful."

She turned away as she took the prosthetic, Krosis coming over to help install the eye. Eve, meanwhile, approches the piles of gold and picks out what appears to be a grenade launcher, the design of a majestic maned creature on either side. With a finger on the trigger guard, she opens the breech and pulls out the loaded shell, Calus turning back to Eve.

Calus; "Ah, a fine piece, that one! Prideglass, a gift from my Sindu shadow."

Eve put the shell back in the breech, closing the weapon and mounting it on her back before looking to Calus with a smile.

Eve; "Thank you, your majesty... But, really, I would like a way to return to Earth, if that's not a problem."

Calus paused a moment before laughing raucously, hands on his knees.

Calus; "Of course, my humble Guardian! Thot'gor can fly you back whenever you feel you are ready. I will make sure Turok sends advance notice of your arrival."

Eve nodded gently with a sigh, mounting the weapon on her back as she turned to look at Netra and Krosis, the latter of whom has pulled a nodule of SIVA from the pile of gold.

Krosis; "Where'd you get this?"

Calus apporached and knelt beside Krosis to watch Eve hold Netras upper hands in her own, Netras outer left eye glowing the same shade of purple as Eves eyes.

Calus; "My Psion scouts have been patrolling the system ever since I arrived. They always have such delectable trinkets to show me."

The Emperor chuckled as Netra gave Eves hands a squeeze, the two of them making eye contact.

Eve; "... Will I see you again?"

Netra let out a breathless chuckle, a smile creasing her cheeks against her rebreather.

Netra; "Heh... I was going to ask you the same thing. Unless something comes up, we'll likely stay on Nessus... Maybe get the chance to live peacefully, if the other crews are going to be occupied with the Red Legion leftovers."

Eve nodded with a smile, bringing a hand up to cup Netrasi- iks cheek, Netra leaning into the Exos touch affectionately.

Eve; "I'll make sure I have time to visit at some point. I promise."

Netras smile widened, bringing a lower hand up to remove her Ether mask, pressing her mandibles to Eves lips, their eyes closing on contact before Netra put the mask back on with a giggle, a baby blue blush on her cheeks.

Netra; "Did I do it right?"

Eve had an open mouth smile afterwards, her thumb tracing soft circles over Netras cheek.

Eve; "Wonderfully, hun."

Evelyn let out a soft sigh, her smile going down as she turned to walk away, her hand lingering in Netras as she proceeded to Thot'gor, whom was juggling a keycard between his fingers like a coin. Turok turned to look at Calus as he watched Thot'gor and Eve leave the vault.

Turok; "What shall I tell the Earth leaders, your eminence?"

Calus stood, holding his hands together in front of his abdomen with a hum.------Calus; "I, Calus, the one true emperor of the Cabal Empire, joyous and generous god that I am, have found and am returning one of your lost to you; A security officer by the name of Evelyn-7, brave warrior and favored of my legion. She has done me a great service by eliminating a rogue... Valus, whose name escapes me. She, and all Guardians of Earth, are welcome to my Leviathan to recieve riches beyond anything they could dream of, if they only choose to earn them. I implore you, join me, and cast your shadow."

Zavala, Cayde, Ikora and Amanda stood around a radio in the Tower Hangar, Cayde letting out a hum as the message ended, Ikora turning to look at him.

Ikora; "This is the Cabal Emperor you mentioned?"

Cayde nodded and folded his arms over his chest.

Cayde; "Sure sounds like him. Ya think he can spare some riches for those of us stuck with a 9-5?"

Ikora shook her head, restraining a smile.

Ikora; "Cayde, this is serious."

Cayde outstretched his arms, almost slapping Amanda in the face.

Cayde; "I am being serious! My job's just as important, where would we be without all that paperwork?"

Amanda pushed Caydes hand down away from her face with a sigh.

Amanda; "Probably a lot better off."

The roar of engines began to fill the hangar as the four turned to see a purple and gold Harvester come to land, transmatting out Eve as Zavala, Cayde and Ikora began to walk over, Cayde practically jogging towards the Harvester.

Cayde; "Wait, riches!"

Just as quickly, the Harvester took off from the Hangar, flying into the stratosphere, prompting Cayde to sag his shoulders with a pout.

Cayde; "Aw."

Zavala looked Evelyn up and down, lingering on her makeshift prosthetics before looking her in the face, holding out a hand that Eve shook with a smile.

Zavala; "Good to have you back, officer. I'm proud to see you've persevered, even without a Ghost."

Eve let out a chuckle, bringing her hands to her sides after the handshake.

Eve; "Can't get rid of me that easily, Commander."

Ikora came over to shake Eves hand, which she did whilst maintaining a smile.

Ikora; "Speaking of Ghosts..."

Coming over from near Amandas workstation was Nolan, who levitated a couple feet away from Evelyn, who had an open mouth smile.

Eve; "Nolan! You're ok!"

Nolan let out a shout as he was grabbed out of the hair by Eve, holding him close to her chest.

Nolan; "Aheh, of course I'm ok kid... I'm sorry about the way I talked to ya. I shouldn't have been so cold."

Eve held out Nolan at arms length before letting him float on his own, nodding with a soft chuckle.

Eve; "It's alright, hun... That water's under the bridge, it's been a long few months."

Zavala clasped his hands behind his back as he spoke, Eve and Nolan turning to look at him.

Zavala; "Eight months to be exact. I believe you've earned some time off, Evelyn... Take a few months to yourself, then I look forward to seeing you get back into the fight."

Eve saluted, and Zavala returned the gesture.

Eve; "Yes, sir. Thank you, sir."

Once his hand went down, Zavala and Ikora turned to walk off while Cayde came over and looked Eves prosthetic legs up and down.

Cayde; "Now, inquiring minds wanna know... Are your old legs gonna come back? Or do you keep these things?"

Eve turned to look out the hangar that overlooked the Last City, looking to Nolan with a smirk.

Eve; "Only one way to find out."

She then sprinted towards the opening, Nolan letting out a sigh and flying after her as she leapt out of the hangar, Nolan following her as she tumbled off the side of the wall, bouncing off of a couple pieces of debris and indentations caused by explosives before landing face down on a dirt road, all of her limbs bent and twisted unnaturally, leaking a black fluid with specks of blue inside. Nolan shook his shell with a mix of amusement and disappointment as his core charged with Light before releasing a shockwave, restoring Eves body, the prosthetics being shucked off and pushed away. Evelyn then rolled herself onto her back as she laughed, resting her hands on her abdomen, looking up at the Traveler as chunks of its shell swirled around it, bound close by light blue Light.

Epilogue

The wave of Light surges across the Sol System, past Nessus and past the Kuiper belt;

Past a world of scrapwork and pink skies, blighted by sickly green fumes and Taken splotches;

Past a planet of pristine white sand and opulent palaces being demolished in favor of brutish military metal and energy;

Past a drifting vessel that hauls a massive spherical object that's on approach to Sol;

Finally stopping at an immense fleet of innumerable black pyramids in space, their hulls lighting up with highlights of orange luster. Deep in the bowels of the ship, a viscous, coal black fluid that girgled and bubbled against the wall of a large room. Emerging from the fluid was a towering figure, relative to the Human-sized veiled statues on either side of the room, their form shimmering as though made of shifting scales that had a mind of their own. Their hands pressed together in front of their abdomen to make the shape of a triangle between their index finger and thumb. Their face was partially obscured by a black collar, only their eyes visible as their head emitted a plume of smoke with myriad faces seen within. The figure approached an opening in the ship, looking out into space where the wave of Light came from.

"No more running away. Finality will be achieved."

With a quick gesture, their pointer finger sticking out and waving to the side, some of the ships in the fleet turned towards the source of the Light shockwave and proceeded at FTL.

"We will not be fooled again. The Final Shape is upon us... And we will suffer your silence no more."

www.ingramcontent.com/pod-product-compliance
Lightning Source LLC
Chambersburg PA
CBHW071022180726
48291CB00004B/1578